"You should not be here. I shouldn't have brought you."

Dara wasn't in the mood for any chauvinistic garbage. "Because women are weak?" she challenged him.

He looked at her for a long moment. "Women should be cherished."

She stared back, unsure what to say to that.

Her father used to say women had to be toughened up to be fit for the military. He hadn't meant it disparagingly. He merely saw the difference between the sexes as a weakness. He was forever frustrated by her mother's inability to hold up under pressure, suck it up and stick it out.

She glanced at Saeed. *Cherished.* It fell so far outside the realm of her experience, she couldn't even picture it. Was he for real?

Dear Harlequin Intrigue Reader,

This July, Intrigue brings you six sizzling summer reads. They're the perfect beach accessory.

* We have three fantastic miniseries for you. *Film at Eleven* continues THE LANDRY BROTHERS by Kelsey Roberts. Gayle Wilson is back with the PHOENIX BROTHERHOOD in *Take No Prisoners*. And B.J. Daniels finishes up her McCALLS' MONTANA series with *Shotgun Surrender*.

* Susan Peterson brings you *Hard Evidence*, the final installment in our LIPSTICK LTD. promotion featuring stealthy sleuths. And, of course, we have a spine-tingling ECLIPSE title. This month's is Patricia Rosemoor's *Ghost Horse*.

* Don't miss Dana Marton's sexy stand-alone title, *The Sheik's Safety*. When an American soldier is caught behind enemy lines, she'll fake amnesia to guard her safety, but there's no stopping the sheik determined on winning her heart.

Enjoy our stellar lineup this month and every month!

Sincerely,

Denise O'Sullivan
Senior Editor
Harlequin Intrigue

THE SHEIK'S SAFETY

DANA MARTON

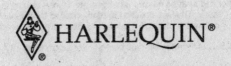

HARLEQUIN®

TORONTO • NEW YORK • LONDON
AMSTERDAM • PARIS • SYDNEY • HAMBURG
STOCKHOLM • ATHENS • TOKYO • MILAN • MADRID
PRAGUE • WARSAW • BUDAPEST • AUCKLAND

To Gail Neeves, a wonderful writer and treasured friend.

With many thanks to Kim Nadelson and Allison Lyons,
the best editors a writer could wish for, and Jenel Looney
for sharing her expertise on Middle Eastern customs
and life, and Anita Staley for her friendship,
help and tireless support.

ISBN 0-373-22859-7

THE SHEIK'S SAFETY

Copyright © 2005 by Marta Dana

www.eHarlequin.com

Printed in U.S.A.

ABOUT THE AUTHOR

Dana Marton lives near Wilmington, Delaware. She has been an avid reader since childhood and has a master's degree in writing popular fiction. When not writing, she can be found either in her large garden or her home library. For more information on the author and her other novels, please visit her Web site at www.danamarton.com.

She would love to hear from her readers via e-mail at DanaMarton@yahoo.com.

Books by Dana Marton

HARLEQUIN INTRIGUE
806—SHADOW SOLDIER
821—SECRET SOLDIER
859—THE SHEIK'S SAFETY

CAST OF CHARACTERS

Dara Alexander—Third-generation military, Dara followed her father's and grandfather's footsteps to the air force before joining a top secret antiterrorist unit, the SDDU. But the desert operation she ends up in this time is more dangerous, with stakes much higher than ever before.

Sheik Saeed ibn Ahmad—Once he was in line for the throne. Now the past is haunting him as he survives one assassination attempt after the other.

Nasir ibn Ahmad—Saeed's brother. He is not happy with Saeed's desire to preserve peace at any cost. Trouble is brewing in the background. Is he the source of it?

King Majid—He came to the throne under suspicious circumstances and would do anything to retain power. But does he want it badly enough to kill his own cousin, Saeed?

Jumaa—The Prime Minister of the country is supposed to hold the real power in a constitutional monarchy. But does he? Is he the king's puppet, or an insidious schemer with his own agenda?

SDDU—Special Designation Defense Unit. A top secret military team established to fight terrorism. Its existence is known only by a select few. Members are recruited from the best of the best, SEALs, FBI and CIA agents, elite military groups.

Colonel Wilson—He's the leader of the SDDU, reporting straight to the Homeland Security Secretary.

Chapter One

They flew below radar, although not as invisible as they would have liked to be.

Dara Alexander took in the starry sky from the cockpit of the MC-130. Not a cloud in sight to cover the moon, no such thing as a pitch-black night here. That was one of the drawbacks of desert missions, and an annoying inconvenience for anyone trying to sneak around.

But the full moon was the least of their worries. They needed only a matter of minutes—fly in low, pop up to safe height for jumping, drop the team, then the plane would go back to base to wait for the pickup signal. Once they were on the ground, being invisible was their specialty.

Dara scanned Beharrain's alien landscape below them, the expanse of rocky plateau broken up by giant boulders every so often, some a couple of hundred feet high. She might as well have been looking at video transmitted back by the Mars Rover. Except that somewhere ahead, a convoy of arms smugglers was heading south, hoping to cross the border to Yemen.

Not today. She rolled her shoulders. Not if her team had anything to do with it.

The pilot looked up from his display—symbology overlaid with sensor video. "Five minutes to drop zone."

"See you in a couple of days." Dara stood and clapped the man on the shoulder to thank him for the ride up front, then smiled at the copilot who was checking the situation data on the instrument panel.

She didn't exactly miss the air force—her current job in the Special Designation Defense Unit, or SDDU, had more than enough excitement—but there was something about sitting in a cockpit that came as close to feeling "home" as she'd ever gotten. She glanced at the navigators and the electronic warfare officer, all three men busy at their console on the aft portion of the flight deck, then she moved on to the back, to the temporary team to which she now belonged.

Joey Scallio flashed her a grin. "How 'bout a kiss for good luck?"

"In your dreams, Scallio."

His grin widened. "Babe, in my dreams we do a hell of a lot more than that."

She shook her head and bit back a smile as she walked on, stretching her legs.

Harrison, their team leader, gave her a thumbs-up and a smile as she walked by him, his perfect white teeth gleaming from his ebony face. He was talking to Miller. "It gets easier after…"

She didn't catch the rest over the noise of the plane. Judging from the proud fatherly smile that spread on the younger man's face, they were probably talking about his newborn son.

She was almost at her seat when the cockpit alarm went off. The shrill tone froze her limbs for a split second.

"Incoming. Surface-to-air missile. Brace for impact," the warning instructed through her headset.

Dara grabbed for one of the belts secured to the wall, twisted it around her arm, and hung on for all she was worth as the plane lurched to the side, the pilot taking evasive action.

Too late.

The plane shook the next second when the SAM hit.

Her right shoulder felt as if it were being ripped out of the socket. More alarms came on, deafening her. She lost hold of the belt and slid across the floor toward the front of the plane. Damn. Fear and adrenaline raced through her veins. She grasped at anything that might hold her, hoping she'd manage before she slammed into the metal crates by the cockpit door and broke a leg. *The cargo net.* She reached for it and succeeded, coming to a halt at last.

She tried to pull up, ignoring the ache in her shoulder, her gaze focused on her nine-millimeter Beretta that had snagged on something and gotten loose as she'd slid. She sought purchase on the floor with her feet, managed to get some leverage and pushed forward.

The plane straightened. Finally. Dara got on her knees to stand, but then the nose of the aircraft lifted and she lurched backward. Her pistol flew out of sight, disappearing behind the guys' feet in the back. Thank God, she'd still had her fingers locked around the net.

She held on tight, her insides trembling.

"They got the left wing." The pilot's voice echoed in her ringing ears. "I'm going to try to pull up. Prepare to jump."

Harrison unbuckled and came for her, helped her parachute on as he hauled her to her feet, opened the door and pushed her out just as she got the last fastener secured. Cold wind hit her in the face, but she barely noticed, floating weightless in the air.

She yanked hard on the rip cord, and the next second the harness bit into her shoulders as the canopy opened and broke her fall. The parachute needed five hundred feet at the minimum to properly operate. She looked down, gauging the distance between herself and the ground. Hard to tell in the dark.

She glanced back at the plane and saw someone

else jump, Miller perhaps, then Scallio, then another. Under optimal circumstances the MC-130 could drop ten men every five seconds. She hoped that would be fast enough.

The second SAM hit.

She stared, a scream of denial frozen on her lips, as the plane exploded. The impact shook the air, the wind of it pushing her back, tangling her suspension lines for a second. She pulled at them frantically as flaming scraps of metal fell from the sky around her to land on the sand and burn on, lighting up the night. Her fall slowed again as the lines twisted free.

She drew a deep breath into her aching lungs and looked up because she couldn't bear to look down. Hers was the only parachute in the air. The other jumpers had been too close.

She rode the slight breeze, numb, her mind struggling to catch up with her eyes. They were dead, all dead. The five officers and four enlisted men of the flight crew, and eleven of the twelve-member SDDU team.

Grief hit her hard, robbing the air from her lungs. But she couldn't afford the luxury of giving in to it, of getting distracted even temporarily.

She was in the middle of hostile territory, alone.

She floated like a lost feather out of the sky, a hundred unrelated thoughts flying through her head. She had no radio contact. Harrison was gone, Miller was gone, and the others…

The ground was coming up to meet her fast. She bent her knees ready for landing, thumped onto the sand, then walked forward to allow her canopy to fold to the ground behind her.

Her gaze hesitated on the faint light on the horizon where the plane was burning. The beacon. Her best chance for rescue was if she stayed as close to her last known location as possible. But the men who had shot down the plane were bound to be there. They had to have seen her jump, which meant they would be looking for her.

Dara glanced at her compass in the moonlight, thought of the map they had studied on the way over.

"Come up with the best plan you can, then give it your best effort. Failure is not an option," she muttered Harrison's favorite mantra aloud.

There was a small village fifty to sixty miles north from where she was now, seventy, tops. Once there, she could sneak in at night to get some water and food, get her hands on a phone or radio and call for help.

She buried her parachute, saving a two-by-four strip to shade her head once the sun came up, then, ignoring her throbbing shoulder, she moved forward at a good clip, away from the plane. She pretended she was on an exercise, that food and water would be waiting for her just beyond the horizon, the guys ribbing her about coming in last.

The guys.

Tears of grief and frustration clouded her eyes. Wouldn't be a problem for long, she thought as she blinked them away. Pretty soon she'd be too dehydrated to cry.

SHEIK SAEED IBN AHMAD IBN Salim ben Zayed scanned his surroundings from the mouth of the cave before he stepped outside into the sunset, careful to note every dune. Two assassination attempts in two weeks had made him cautious.

His sharp whistle brought his black stallion trotting over. "Time to go, Hawk."

He vaulted himself into the saddle, grabbed his flask, and drank the last of his water. He could refill at the oasis halfway between here and camp. He capped the flask and glanced back at the opening of the cave, anger still at a slow boil in his gut. Whatever it took, he would find the thieves.

The treasure belonged to his tribe, the knowledge of it passed down through the centuries from sheik to sheik—father to son. In times of dire need, when the livelihood of the tribe was threatened, the sheik would take enough to last them until the drought lifted and famine passed.

The cave's secret had been their thousand-year-old disaster insurance. Allah be thanked, they hadn't needed it in the last couple of decades, not since oil income from the tribe's southern territories became dependable. They made it through the twelve-year drought of the eighties and early nineties without having to touch the gold. But it was theirs just the same, their heritage. No one knew what the future might bring.

At least the thieves hadn't taken everything. The cave, continuing for hundreds of meters underground, had many crevices, the treasure carefully concealed. Only a small cache had been broken into, close to the entrance. Not a significant loss, a million dollars' worth or so.

But once it was spent, they would be back hoping for more. And that he couldn't allow. He couldn't let them find the passageway leading underground. He either had to figure out a way to guard the treasure or move it.

A sudden squall threw sand into his face, and he leaned forward in the saddle as Hawk flew across the distance. He had to come up with a plan, or his enemies would bury him faster than a windstorm. He watched the desert for any sign of danger as he rode. And then he saw it.

A man lying ahead to the right in ambush.

Saeed ducked in the saddle and turned Hawk, urged him faster, but no shots rang out. He rode on until he knew he was out of sight then circled back, sick of the game and ready to bring it to an end.

The previous assassins had been killed by his angry tribesmen before he'd had the chance to question them. He needed one alive. He had a fair idea of who had paid the men, but he needed proof—a confession he could take to the Council of Ministers.

He left Hawk out of sight and bade him to stay, came in on foot, then on his belly over the last dune. The man wasn't moving. At all. Nobody who knew anything about the desert would have lain down in the sand like that, exposed to the elements, to sleep. And stranger yet, no sign of how he had gotten there, no camel or horse or car.

Saeed crept closer, his gun ready as he made his way over to the prone figure with caution, all the while watching out for more of them, for any sign of ambush. When he came within twenty feet or so, he stood and shouted a greeting. The man, lying face down in the sand, didn't move. Dead, he thought and went closer yet. The stranger's back rose and sank, the slight movement barely noticeable.

"Get up."

The man didn't move a muscle, made no attempt to even look at him.

With rifle in hand, ready for any surprise, Saeed flipped him over with the tip of his foot. The stranger made no sound, nor did he open his eyes. He was unarmed, save a knife he kept in a holster on his thigh, of which Saeed relieved him at once. He wore a camouflage uniform with no military markings, his face wrapped against the sun. A lone bandit, probably a mercenary. His proximity to the cave was more than suspicious.

Was he one of the thieves who had stolen the gold? Or was he another would-be assassin? He reached down to pull off the frayed headdress, but the knot in the back was too tight. Time enough for that later. Saeed whistled for Hawk, and when the stallion trotted over, he lifted the listless stranger in front of the saddle then mounted the horse. He had to make sure the man lived long enough to answer his questions.

The stallion rode as if sensing the urgency, paying no heed to the extra weight—not that the man was heavy, rather the opposite. Must have been out in the desert without food and water for some time. He was lucky. Weather had been mild and temperate this January so far. Had it been summer, he would have been already dead.

THEY REACHED THE OASIS in two hours or so, a couple of stars already visible in the sky. The place wasn't much more than a seasonal watering hole with a handful of scraggly date palms and a smattering of grasses.

Saeed slid out of the saddle, caught the stranger when the man nearly fell after him, and lowered the limp body to the sand. He used the man's knife to slice through the knot of the headdress in the back, wanting to free his mouth to get some water into him.

He turned him with his left hand, the knife in his right. Then stopped in midmotion.

His left palm, having tried to brace the stranger's chest, was filled with a mound of flesh, soft and round. He was old enough to recognize a female breast, especially one that filled his palm to perfection as this one did.

Allah be merciful...

She was beautiful in the moonlight, despite the grime that had found its way under the fabric. Her hair, the color of rich, spiced coffee, had half escaped from the braid that had once contained it. For a moment the face of another woman appeared before him, her black curls streaming to the ground as she lay dying in his arms.

He blinked away the memory and focused on the foreigner. Her feminine, delicate features stood in puzzling contrast to the uniform she wore.

A female soldier? Israel had women in its army; so did the U.S.A. But what would one be doing here? Judging from her exotic features, she was a westerner. He unbuttoned the top two buttons of her shirt and reached inside.

The back of his hand brushed against velvet skin. He hesitated for a moment before continuing.

No dog tags.

His first assessment had been correct. She did not belong to the military. But then who was she? He had a hard time believing her proximity to the cave was a coincidence. She had to be there either for him or for the gold.

He walked over to the well, shook the bucket clean and lowered it, relieved when he heard the unmistakable sound of it hitting water instead of mud. The water was full of sand as expected, but better than nothing at all. He used the woman's makeshift head-dress to strain water into his flask, then went to settle onto the sand by her side.

He dribbled water onto her parched lips, and when she moaned, he sloshed some into her mouth, massaging her graceful neck, helping her to swallow. "Drink."

His eyes settled on the small triangle of skin between her collarbones revealed by the top two open buttons. Her pale skin shone in the moonlight. If she was a mercenary, a hired assassin, they had picked well this time.

This one could have gotten to him.

He helped her drink some more, folded the wet cloth and placed it on her forehead, then went back to the well to draw water for Hawk and considered whether to unsaddle him while they rested.

"Sorry, friend." He patted the stallion's neck, deciding he could not afford to give the animal that comfort. "We might have to leave in a hurry."

He strained the water for the horse as carefully as he had for the woman, but still when Hawk tasted it, he shook his head a couple of times.

"You'll get a cleaner drink when we get to camp."

Hawk bent to the bucket as if understanding, but looked up after a few moments, his ears turning. He picked up his head and neighed.

Saeed listened to the night. Nothing. Then he could hear it too, a low rumbling sound. He stood and searched the desert until he spotted the source: a black SUV coming at them from behind, flying over the sand. Moonlight glinted off the rifle barrels that hung out each window.

Here we go again. By Allah, he was tired of this game. And he had no choice but to play it out to the end.

He pulled the woman under the cover of two palms that grew side by side, their twin trunks offering sufficient protection.

He glanced at Hawk, out in the open, and let out a sharp whistle that sent the stallion galloping off into the desert to safety just as the first series of shots rang out.

He peered from behind the palm and took aim. The rifle flew out of the driver's hand the next second. Somewhat of an improvement, as now only three of them were shooting, but the SUV picked up speed, the man's full attention on driving now.

Saeed had his great-grandfather's bolt-action Remington, a finely made piece, but still only eight rounds, no more. He had to pick his aim carefully. The next shot shattered the windshield, the one after that hit the radiator. Steam rose from under the hood but the vehicle didn't halt.

It didn't even slow.

He aimed again and hit the man in the passenger seat, then squeezed off another round, trying for the driver. The SUV veered to the left as it came to a slow halt on the sand.

The two men in the back got out and hid behind the open doors for a minute before throwing themselves to the ground.

Using the tufts of grass for cover, Saeed crawled along a natural indentation in the sand, moving as fast as he dared toward the well. Its raised stone edge, about half a meter high, offered more substantial protection, and if he managed to reach it without being detected he might be able to pick off the men from the side.

He made it—a miracle—squeezed off a shot, ducked down again. Return fire came swiftly. He kept quiet, waiting for them to get closer. He could not afford to miss. No margin for error. Zero. He was down to his last two bullets.

He peered from his cover then ducked back when they shot at him. The men had separated, circling the well one on each side. He would be in the line of fire soon. He rolled into the open, aimed, shot, rolled back.

One attacker remained.

Saeed lay low to the ground, waited until the man came into sight—rifle first, holding the AK-47 extended before him. With his last bullet, Saeed shot at the right arm then pulled back immediately. A shout of pain and rage flew across the sand. Good. He wanted him incapacitated but alive. He wanted answers.

He took off his kaffiyeh and wrapped it around the Remington's barrel then lifted it above the rim of the well.

No shots.

He stuck his head out. The man was rolling back and forth, grasping his wrist.

"I will pay the blood price in gold," Saeed said as he walked to him. "For the name of the one who sent you, I will pay double."

The man looked at him with death in his eyes and lifted his rifle with his good arm.

Even though the assassin was too far, Saeed grabbed his dagger and charged forward, prepared for the bite of bullets, knowing the certainty of death but wanting to go out fighting. He was the sheik, he would not shame his people by dying from a bullet in the back that he'd gotten while running from his enemy. He thought of his family and hoped he had time for a quick prayer for them.

He could clearly see the man's finger on the trigger, the small movement of the last two digits as he began to squeeze it. *Allah be merciful.*

Something hissed in the air. The next thing he knew, the man was facedown in the sand, a knife sticking out of his back.

Where had that come from? Saeed drew up short. Movement by the palm trees caught his gaze, and he stared at the moonlit figure of the woman standing with her feet braced apart. Her long hair streamed around her shoulders, flitting in the strengthening breeze.

His captive was awake.

SHE HOPED TO HELL she had made the right decision. Because now that she had thrown her spare knife, she was officially unarmed. Dara rubbed her right shoulder as she took in the surprise on the man's face, visible in the full moon even at this distance.

They were at an oasis, although she had no clue how she'd gotten there. She had come to in the middle of a gunfight and her first thought—after she'd pushed back the sudden rush of memories of the crash and the onslaught of grief—was to sneak off unseen. Then she spotted the SUV.

The vehicle was worth staying for. But she couldn't make a beeline for it with three men filling the air with bullets. She contented herself with watching the fight, hoping they would kill each other and save her the unpleasant trouble.

The one with the blue headdress wasn't half-bad, but woefully outmatched by the two with AK-47s. The decision to save him hadn't been conscious. Instinct had whipped her arm forward when she threw the knife, instinct honed by years of combat experience.

She watched, wary now, as the man started toward her, his heavy dark robe parting to show a long white shirt that reached almost to the bottom of his white pants. He finished rewrapping his headdress as he walked, leaving only his eyes free. She assessed him, trying to determine how much of a threat he was.

His figure trim and muscular, he walked steady and didn't appear wounded. He looked to be in his midthirties, a couple of years older than she was, a man in his prime. None of her observations pleased her. Least of all that he was armed.

She locked her trembling knees as he came nearer. Under no circumstances did she want him to know how weak she was. She glanced at the vehicle. Too far. She didn't have enough strength to run. She looked around for a makeshift weapon and came up empty. Great. She really hoped the guy felt some gratitude for her saving his life, because judging by his size and the state she was in currently, no way she could wrestle him down.

Ah, hell. She wasn't supposed to come into contact with anyone except for the arms smugglers they were here to pick up. The Colonel had high hopes they'd talk if put under enough stress, and lead him to Tsernyakov, the elusive businessman who was responsible for eighty percent of the illegal gun trade in the region.

No one was supposed to know about the unauthorized U.S. military operation in the country. From the look of him, the guy striding toward her had a couple of questions. She wracked her brain for a logical explanation on what she was doing in the middle of the desert in a camouflage uniform.

He stopped a few feet from her, a silver-studded antique rifle slung over his shoulder. He had her two knives tucked into his belt, his sinister curved dagger still in hand. The light of the full moon glinted off the dagger's golden sheath that looked like a museum piece.

She raised her gaze to the man's face, hoping to read his intention. "Where am I?"

The cobalt blue of the headdress matched his eyes that appraised her with curiosity and distrust. What little skin she could see looked tanned by the sun, his eyelashes and eyebrows the blackest black. He looked fierce and proud, a warrior from another time.

"Jabrid," he said.

She hoped that was the name of the oasis and not Arabic for "prepare to die."

The intensity of his gaze was unnerving. Scenes from a long-ago-seen movie floated through her mind, about a desert prince coming upon an English woman, the sole survivor of a caravan attack, throwing her over his horse and carrying her off to his sumptuous tent. She could swear the man in front of her was the guy. Except, no horse, she noted with relief. And then, without taking his eyes off her, he whistled.

The brief series of notes was not earsplitting, but high-pitched and swift, carrying over the sand. She turned in the direction of a soft sound coming from behind her, and what she saw took her breath away.

The magnificent black stallion coming toward them was straight out of the film. His long mane and tail swept through the air, his saddle covered with a richly woven blanket—red and white, she could just make out the colors in the moonlight—the tassel fringe bobbing like so many tiny bells. A white mark, in the distinct form of a bird spreading its wings in flight, graced the animal's forehead.

"Do you have any more knives?" the man asked with a British accent, drawing her attention from the horse, which came to a stop next to him and was now nuzzling his wide shoulders.

The muscle cramps in her legs were strong enough to make her knees buckle, but she bit her lips and thrust out her chin, refusing to fall down. She lifted her hands a little, palms forward. "Fresh out."

He looked her over then nodded, slid his dagger into its sheath. "Who are you?"

"That's the million-dollar question, isn't it?" She widened her smile, trying to look innocent.

His eyes narrowed. "You want a million for the answer?"

She laughed. Never let them see you scared. "I meant I'd give a million if anyone could tell me."

He took a few seconds to digest that. "You don't remember?" he asked with a hint of incredulity, one ebony eyebrow cocked.

"Nothing before I woke up under this palm to the sound of shooting."

"Nothing?" The second eyebrow joined the first.

Her lips pressed together in mock consternation, she shook her head. Shouldn't have done that, she realized as the landscape swam around her. Three days of forced march through the desert without food and water had left her severely dehydrated. She swayed a little, but caught herself. He must not know what an easy prey she was.

He made an unintelligible sound as he looked her over again. "You sound American."

No sense in denying that, since her unmistakable accent had already given her away. "Yes, I think so."

"Why were you armed?"

"I don't know."

"Where did you get the second knife from?"

She glanced down and pointed at her boot.

"And you're sure you don't have any more?"

"I don't think I do."

"I'd like to check."

She thoroughly resented the suggestion. Could be worse though—he could have demanded a strip search. In her current condition, she was pretty much obliged to do whatever he asked. Well…within reason. She plopped onto the sand, grateful to be off her feet. A few more minutes and she would have fallen. Maybe if she played nice, he would let her have some food and water, not to mention the SUV. He didn't need the vehicle anyhow. He had his horse.

She took off her boots and tossed them to him, then while he looked them over, she took off her socks, too, enjoying the air on her feet, reluctant to put her footgear back on when he returned it.

"Any water in that well?" She nodded toward the stone circle with her head. Her tongue felt swollen, her lips painfully chapped.

"Too much sand in it," he said as he pulled a flask from the saddlebag and handed it to her, his eyes narrowing once again, as if he were trying to decide what to do with her.

She gulped the gritty liquid, holding onto the flask with both hands, prepared to fight for it if he tried to take it away.

"We're a few hours ride from camp, plenty of clean water there," he said.

Tempting, but no. She met his dagger-sharp gaze. She was definitely not going to some desert bandit camp with him.

Chapter Two

"I need to get to the nearest town." She drank the grainy water to the last drop, smiled at him as she laced up her boots. "I'd like to get in touch with the American embassy. Do you think I could take the car?"

"You're not well enough to go anywhere alone."

"You could…escort me?"

He waited a while before responding. "Tihrin is too far. I'll take you to the camp, then when you're better, I'll take you to Tihrin."

"I'm really pretty good." She stood, and prayed he didn't notice the slight wobble. She had to get to a phone. She had to tell the Colonel what had happened to the team.

"In a few days." He whistled for the horse again, lower this time as the animal was nearby. "Right now, we'll be safer at the camp."

Right. Because he looked safe. Not. "Why don't you ride the horse and I'll drive the car and follow you?"

"We leave the car."

She needed some time to come up with a plan. "Mind if we rest a little before we go? I'm not sure I'm up for horseback riding yet."

He glanced at the bodies behind him then back at her. "A few minutes," he said. "There might be more of them coming."

He was just full of good news. She wondered if the four dead men were in any way connected to whomever had shot down the plane. Where was an M4 when she needed one? "Can I have my knives back?"

"No."

Not very accommodating, was he? "In case there's another attack?"

He shook his head. "I will protect you."

For a moment she considered reminding him who had saved whose life, but decided against it. No sense in appearing too contrary, no point in raising any suspicions.

He took a few steps toward the bodies on the sand, stopped and turned back. "What is your name?"

"I don't remember."

"I'm Saeed," he said, and left her.

She watched him as he went from one body to the next, checking them over, coming up empty-handed as far as she could tell. It took all her strength to make her way to the horse a few short feet away.

"Come on, boy." She let the animal smell her, patted his head. "What a fine horse you are."

Purebred Arabian. She remembered her grandfather's horses on the reservation, a couple of pintos and a half dozen wild mustangs he'd bought through the government program. They were all beautiful in their right. But this one—this one was a prince.

"Here we go." She moved to his side and checked to make sure the cinch was good and tight. When she tried to put her foot in the stirrups the animal danced away.

"You're not scared of me, are you?" She kept on talking, utter nonsense in a calming voice, as she tried again. Same result. Horses were supposed to be in her blood. Apparently, someone forgot to tell this one. The stallion had been trained, and trained well. Figured.

"Tayib, hoah."

The deep voice coming from behind startled her, but seemed to calm the horse. Saeed stepped forward and grabbed the bridle.

"You can get on now," he said, four AK-47s slung over his shoulder.

For a split second, she considered fighting him for the guns.

His gaze was sharp on her face, steady. She could barely stand. If she didn't succeed, what would he do? Kill her, leave her to die in the desert or tie her up and take her to his camp anyway? She had to face the truth—she could not overtake him. To try would accomplish nothing but tip her hand and make escape more difficult later.

She mounted, and as soon as she was in the saddle, he vaulted up behind her. His arms, one on each side of her now, held onto the rein and set the horse going with a gentle flick.

As if the moving animal had unbalanced her, she slid to the side, testing Saeed. His arm barely moved, although she'd leaned her full weight against it.

He was strong and in control of his strength. In control of her, too, for the moment. As temporary as it was, she didn't like the feeling. Dara straightened herself in the saddle. He was taking her, whether she wanted to go with him or not.

Fine. She would ride to his camp, eat, get her hands on a few flasks of water, then sneak away at the first opportunity. Shouldn't set her back more than a day.

SAEED KEPT HIS EYES on the desert, constantly scanning the horizon, unsure when or from where the next ambush would come, knowing only that they weren't done with him yet.

The woman in front of him had made a valiant effort of staying upright when they'd first mounted, but was now sagging farther back in the saddle, losing her strength rapidly. Her back touched his chest and she jerked forward, but soon was slipping again.

He let go of the rein with his left hand to pull her fully against him, leaving his arm around her waist to hold her in place, unsure how much longer she could do it on her own. "Rest."

"I'm fine," she said, but didn't pull away.

She felt frail in his arms, but he knew better. She had survived several days in the open desert, taken out an armed assassin with a knife from forty meters. Helpless she was not.

And yet, despite knowing she was probably part of whatever band of thieves had robbed his tribe, he could not quench the surge of protective feelings inside him. Probably because she was a woman, in his arms.

It had been a while since he'd held anyone. Although her head was covered with her makeshift headdress once again, it would be some time before he would forget her face and the way she had looked at him. Her eyes shone like jewels—black onyx with freckles of gold.

She felt soft in all the right places, all sinuous muscle in others. Her shapely behind wedged between his thighs moved against him slightly to the rhythm of the horse, bringing thoughts to his mind the likes of which he had been too busy to think for far too long.

He brought his focus back to more pressing issues. "Where are the rest of your people?"

She stiffened. "I don't remember anyone."

Hard to say if she was lying or not. He would have expected a foreign woman who found herself in the desert in the middle of a gunfight with no idea of how she'd gotten there to be a little more frazzled. Maybe she was in shock, too numb for hysterics. No. Not shock. She had thrown that knife with precision, good and steady. And she appeared fine, save her weakness from exposure and lack of food and water. And of course lack of memory—if she wasn't faking that.

With his attackers dead, once again she was the only possible source of information he had. As much as she wanted to reach Tihrin, he could not let her go until he found out for whom she worked and what her purpose was here.

She shivered in his arms.

"Here." He slipped off his kaffiyeh, wrapped it around her head, neck and shoulders as best as he could. "Before today you don't remember anything?" He tried again.

Her response came slower than before. "Nothing. I think maybe I got lost."

He chewed on that for a while.

She wasn't an assassin. She could have let that man shoot him or, for that matter, she could have buried that knife in his chest just as easily as she'd done in the attacker's back. But if she wasn't in league with the assassins, chances were she was in league with the thieves. Her proximity to the cave when he had found her certainly pointed in that direction.

She had come to steal from him, then had a fallout with her partners in crime who'd left her in the desert for dead. If that was the case, she could hardly reveal her identity to anyone. But with time, if she came to trust him... For a suitable reward she might be willing to give up those who had betrayed her.

But not anytime soon. She was completely limp in his arms. He tightened his hold on her to make sure she wouldn't slip out of the saddle now that she was out again.

The wadi they rode in deepened, until he could no longer see out. He didn't mind. If someone drove across the sand at a distance they wouldn't see him, but he would be able to hear the noise of their motor. And they were close to camp now. That, too, made him more comfortable.

Soon he would be able to see the small rocky *jebel*, not even a hill but more of a tall outcropping of stones, that protected the encampment from the wind on the east side. A small path led down, steep but doable. Hawk could manage just about any terrain.

He turned the horse up the familiar incline when they reached it. Another few feet and they were high enough so he could see over the bank. And saw the men. He pulled on Hawk's rein, and without a word, made the horse retreat, then stopped him when he was sure they were back out of sight again. There were people on the ledge above the encampment, two Jeeps with seven men that he had counted.

Not his people.

Had he been alone, he would have crept closer to investigate; as it was, he had to go around, miles out of his way, to get all the way behind the camp without being seen.

He managed, pushing Hawk more than he should have, worried he might lose the stranger in his arms.

DARA STARED at the enormous weaving to her left that hung from the black ceiling of the opulent tent, dividing it in half. Willing the pain in her shoulder to go away, she let her gaze glide over the vibrant colors that made up the slightly off, ornate pattern in the badly woven material. She had fleeting memories of a woman, wrapped in black from head to toe, bending over her. What happened to her?

Sunlight filtered through the cloth panels, the voices of distant chatter coming from outside. Déjà vu. She shook her head to clear it of the memories of summers she had spent on the reservation when she was young. She had loved her mother's Lenape heritage as a small child, hated it as a teenager, denied it as an adult. Maybe if her mother hadn't abandoned her father and her when she was twelve, it would have been different.

She sealed off the thought and the feelings it brought with practiced ease and sat up, noticing for the first time the indigo dress of fine linen that reached to her ankles. And panicked. Somebody had dressed her, which meant she'd been undressed first. The voices rose outside. Women. There were women around. She relaxed and straightened her dress, letting her fingers glide over the soft material. It had been a while since she had worn one. She was used to army fatigues.

Because she was a soldier, she reminded herself, annoyed because she liked the dress. She didn't miss that kind of stuff. Didn't need it. She stood and looked around. She had the skills to get out of here with or without help, trained for not only fight but escape and evasion. Other than her shoulder and a mild burning sensation around her right eye, she was fine.

Kilim carpets covered some of the sand; colorful bags hung from the tent posts; a handful of large pots and pans lay around the ashes of the cooking fire. A strange loom stretched to her right, a half-finished black-and-red cloth on it. She looked for a weapon. A small kitchen knife would have done. Nothing.

She rubbed her right eye, her stomach growling. God, she was hungry. And thirsty. She glanced at the plastic containers in the corner and hoped they held water.

Some kind of funky butter in the first, tea leaves in the second, an aromatic spice in the third. She popped the lid off the last one and sighed in relief.

The water going down her throat felt like heaven. She drank as much as she dared and stopped far from being satisfied. She was in the middle of the desert. When she left, she had to take as much water with her as she could.

She remembered the men at the oasis, the fight, Saeed. She needed to figure out where she was, get her hands on some food and water, borrow or steal a car, or at least a horse. She wasn't sure she could manage a camel, but if it came to that, she'd sure as hell try.

Voices rose and fell outside like music. She could make contact and hope they were friendly and would help her with supplies, or sneak away before anyone realized she had come to. She looked through a small gap in the outer panel of the tent where time had loosened the threads of the weaving.

She could see another dozen tents from her vantage point, a couple of men around an open fire, armed as if for war, with bullet-studded belts looped over their shoulders and rifles lying across their knees or in the sand next to them.

A sudden noise behind her made her spin around into a crouch, ready to fight.

A small boy of five or so stood by the tent divider,

wearing a colorful dress, his large brown eyes rounded at the sight of her. She straightened and smiled, not wanting to scare him.

He watched her with open curiosity, unruly black curls framing his head, gold glinting at his ears. After a few seconds of perusal, he spoke in Arabic.

Dara smiled and shook her head. "I don't understand."

"I'm Salah. Are you my new teacher?"

"No," she said.

His big brown eyes rounded even larger. "Is my father going to marry you?"

"Absolutely not. I'm just visiting."

He visibly relaxed. "That's what Fatima said. She says Father will marry for alliance between the tribes. He can't marry a foreigner. It wouldn't be any use at all."

Dara blinked at so much practicality coming from such a little person. Who was Fatima? Probably one of the boy's father's wives.

"Is your father Saeed?"

The boy nodded.

The fact that there were women and children around set her at ease. She didn't think it would be so at a renegade terrorist camp. Saeed had saved her life by carrying her out of the desert. And he had said he would help her to get to the city once she was better. She would just have to convince him she was better now. She had no time to waste.

"Can you take me to your father, Salah?"

The child shook his head. "He's with the elders. I'll call Fatima and Lamis and then he can talk to you when he comes back."

Of course. Although Beharrain was a progressive country, in most regions the old traditions held fast. Women did not keep company with men unless they were related. She had read the culture advisory report, all twenty pages of its dos and don'ts before deployment.

"Thank you," she said. "I'd like that."

The child ran off, and Dara stepped to one of the tent poles, felt around inside the woven bags that hung from it. Clothes, yarn, some funky tools she couldn't recognize—maybe for cooking or weaving—none of them suitable as a weapon. Damn it. She needed to be ready in case she couldn't bring Saeed around to take her to Tihrin right away. She needed food and water, transportation, and weapons for self-defense.

She stepped away from the bags a split second before two young women came in, one around twenty, the other a year or two younger, introducing themselves as Fatima and Lamis. They wore beautiful dresses, one purple, one dark green with gold thread designs. They brought food and water, and set it in front of her.

"How are you?" Fatima, the older one, asked with a pronounced accent. She was stunning. Her ebony hair reached to the middle of her back, visible through the sheer black scarf that covered it. "Please let me know if you don't like this." She pointed to the tray of food. "I can bring something else."

Dara sat by the plate when the women did, and gave herself points for not tackling them and diving for the food as soon as they'd come through the flap. "Thank you." She reached for a piece of fruit first, a thick slice of melon, wanting to ease her stomach into eating, trying to avoid being sick.

The melon juice tasted like honey, its aromatic flavor flooding her taste buds. Tears sprung to her eyes at the relief of having food again. Until this moment, no matter how much she had refused to let herself think of it, she hadn't been sure she would survive. And still, it was a long way to the city yet. She reached for a boiled egg. Protein. She needed that to regain her strength.

When she finished eating, Fatima rummaged through one of the woven bags and brought over a black scarf and handed it to her.

"Thank you." Dara ran her fingers through her hair, surprised to find it washed and combed. "When did I come here?"

Fatima looked at her with surprise on her face. "Yesterday. Our brother found you in the desert."

Our brother. They were Saeed's sisters. She wondered where the little boy's mother was. She fumbled with the scarf. A mirror would have helped.

Lamis came over, took the sheer material from her and secured it with ease. "It is our custom to cover our hair."

"But not your face?" Dara thought of the images she'd seen on TV.

"Not our tribe. It is different in every region. When we're in the desert we follow the tribal customs, when we're in the city, we follow the customs of the city. There we cover everything. Wahhabism." She made a face as she said the word, then leaned back to survey her handiwork. "Very pretty." She smiled.

"Thank you."

The little boy ran in, stared at Dara for a moment, said something in Arabic, then ran out.

Fatima rose. "Our brother is ready to see you." She stepped to the divider, parted it and stepped through first, holding it for Dara.

She followed, ready to make her case, to bargain or manipulate, whatever would be needed. Then she saw Saeed. He sat cross-legged in front of the glowing embers of a fire.

His headdress rested in a relaxed loop around his neck now, his face uncovered. *Kaboom.* His cobalt-blue eyes shone from his tanned face, above the straight nose and masculine lips. Strength and power radiated from him like heat and light from the fire. He had a paralyzing effect on her. She could hear blood rush in her ears, loudly like a waterfall. She was *not* going to faint. She pressed her short nails into her palm. God, this was ridiculous. Her reaction to the man was absurd.

Fatima and Lamis sat, and she sank onto the carpet next to them, the air leaving her lungs with a whoosh as a strange sensation sucked in like quicksand every coherent thought in her mind. The rest of the tent dimmed then began to spin slowly. The food, she thought. She had eaten too much too fast. She held fast to his piercing gaze, clear and steady.

"I'm glad to see you're feeling better." His deep voice filled the tent as well as her chest cavity.

She nodded, unable to form words. If only he knew.

"Exposure can tax the body," he said.

Of course. That was why she was feeling so discombobulated. She needed to drink more, eat enough to regain her strength.

"Have you remembered anything?" His gaze was mesmerizing.

"No," she croaked out her first word at last, and hoped to hell it sounded convincing.

He nodded. "You will stay here until you do."

"No." The protest flew from her lips. "Thank you for your hospitality." She tried to temper it, to give him a good, logical reason. "I need to contact the embassy as soon as possible. There might be people worried about me."

He gave her a long, hard look.

She pushed on. "How far are we from Tihrin, the town you mentioned?"

"About three hundred kilometers. What is your name?"

"I don't remember." He'd asked her that before. Was he trying to trip her up?

"I can help you hide from those who seek to harm you."

His words sounded sincere. Too bad she had no idea what he was getting at. Did he know about the plane crashing? Was whoever shot it down hunting her? All the more reason to get to Tihrin fast. "Thank you," she said. *I think.*

"There are those who seek to harm me. A friend who might lead me to my enemies would prove a good friend indeed and would be well rewarded," he went on.

Huh? The oasis. Did he think she knew the men who had attacked him? "I would help you if I could."

This much was true. She did not wish to see him dead.

Voices rose outside the tent, men yelling.

"When your memory returns, I want to be told at once." He sat without moving, his gaze not leaving her for a second. Indeed, it had not left her since she had come in.

A woman called out and Dara glanced in the direction of the voice, realizing for the first time that the entrance flap of the tent was open to the outside. Saeed responded in Arabic and the woman stepped in, carrying a pail.

"This is Shadia. She took care of you when you arrived," Saeed said. "She wishes to take care of your eye infection."

Dara rubbed her eye. Eye infection. Great. Damn this stupid sand that got in everywhere and irritated everything.

The woman, her clothes worn but clean, settled down next to her, dipped a scrap of wool into the dark yellow liquid in the pail.

And then Dara got a whiff of it. "What's that?"

The intensity on Saeed's face relaxed into watchfulness, with some humor glinting around his eyes. "Camel urine. It's a very strong disinfectant."

Okay then. She came to her feet startling the woman. "No, thank you."

"She already treated you with it several times when you were unconscious."

Dara made a note not to pass out ever again as long as she lived. People did weird stuff to you, abusing your weakness.

"Thank you." She bowed to the woman. "I'm much better now."

Shadia looked confused, then shook her head with

disapproval when Saeed translated, but picked up her bucket and left the tent.

Dara sat back down. *Close call with camel urine averted.* What else had they done to her while she was out? She had a feeling she didn't want to know.

"Shadia is a very competent servant," Saeed said. "You can trust yourself to her. If the eye gets worse, you *will* have to do something to treat it."

"I'll make sure to see a doctor in Tihrin." She stared at the hint of a grin that hovered over his masculine lips. The man had a mouth to die for.

He looked toward the tent's opening and she followed his gaze, watching a man approach. His brother, she knew without being told. Saeed looked like some ancient Bedouin warlord, terror of the caravans. The younger man who entered the tent looked smoother, boyishly handsome instead of ruggedly so, like an actor Hollywood would choose to play Saeed's role in the movie made about him.

He greeted Saeed without taking his eyes off her. That was different, too—his irises were golden brown instead of blue. They shone with intensity as he took her in.

Saeed said something to him. He didn't respond.

"My brother, Nasir," he said then.

Nasir nodded to her, said something to Saeed that made him stand.

"I must leave. Welcome to our tent. If you need

anything, you need only to ask one of my sisters." He stepped through the flap and after a few moments called back for Nasir.

And then, the younger man finally dropped his gaze from her face and reluctantly left.

Phew. Double whammy. Dara took a giant breath and felt the air flood her lungs. She had barely breathed while the men were in there. Fatima and Lamis stood, so she did, too, registering for the first time this side of the tent. The divider looked stunning from here. It wasn't badly woven as she'd first thought, but had the good side toward the men's section.

Carpets covered most of the sand, except for around the fire. An ancient curved sword hung from one of the poles. She made a mental note of that. Better than nothing.

A strange contraption sat in the corner. A camel saddle, she realized after a moment. She spotted two ammunition belts as she turned, but no guns. Then she didn't have the chance to gawk any longer as both Fatima and Lamis were already on the other side of the divider, expecting her to follow them.

She went straight to the carpet and blankets she'd woken up on, sat and ate the remainder of her food, drank some water and lay down. She had to regain her full strength then get to town. If an opportunity didn't present itself, she'd create one.

She kept her eyes closed, pretending to sleep, not

wanting to be bothered, and especially not wanting to be asked any questions she was not at liberty to answer.

The women chatted on in the corner, paying little mind to her. Good. She needed time to think up a plan.

DARA OPENED HER EYES and peered around in the dark tent, listening to the sound of gentle snoring somewhere nearby. A moment later when her eyes adjusted to the darkness, she could see the lone sleeping figure by the outer wall of the tent. Shadia, the servant woman.

She better not have—Dara rubbed her eyes with her fingers, sniffed them. No suspicious odor. Good. Shadia hadn't done anything disgusting to her while she'd slept. Which was fortunate for everyone around. Because although she'd shown amazing restraint and politeness this afternoon, not wanting to offend her host, if somebody came near her with a bucket of camel urine again, she was ready to defend herself.

She sat up, careful not to make a sound. Now that her body was rehydrated and she had food in her stomach, she was close to being back to her full strength. The rest helped, too. She was ready—if not for leaving, at least for a small reconnaissance mission. Although, if she came across a vehicle she could grab, she was out of here.

She rose little by little, arranged the blankets to show a lump in case Shadia woke and looked her way. Barefoot, she crept toward the spot where the wall carpets overlapped, separated them silently and peeked through to Saeed's side. The flap was closed, this section of the tent as dark as the other.

The sword was gone from the pole.

Saeed didn't trust her. She couldn't blame him.

Her eyes settled on a briefcase by the tent's outer wall. It hadn't been there before. She moved forward silently, stopped and listened before squatting down. She pressed her palm against the lock to muffle the sound as she pushed the button. The metal clasp sprang open against her skin with a barely audible click. She let it up slowly.

The briefcase's lid opened without a sound, and she rummaged through the contents, identifying them as much by feel as sight in the dimness of the tent. Files, a couple of letters—their envelopes previously opened—a satellite phone. Her fingers closed around the latter. She stopped to listen for anyone approaching from outside. Nothing.

She flipped the phone open and turned it on, dialed the Colonel's number, held her breath at the series of beeps, but the servant woman's snoring remained steady. The phone rang on the other side. What time was it there? Midafternoon, she guessed. Then finally the Colonel came on the line.

Cupping her left hand around the phone and her mouth, she whispered her identifying number for this mission.

"Are you all right?"

"Yes, sir."

"The others? We've had no contact."

"No, sir." She swallowed, and told him about the crash.

"What is your location?"

"I'm not sure, sir. I'm at some kind of a Bedouin camp, three hundred kilometers from Tihrin. The clan leader is someone by the name of Saeed."

"Sheik Saeed ibn Ahmad?"

Sheik? She swallowed again, pulled an envelope from the briefcase and held it up to the meager light the phone's LCD provided. The addresses were in Arabic. She picked up another, the same. The third had come from England, bearing careful lettering she finally recognized. *Sheik Saeed ibn Ahmad ibn Salim ben Zayed.* "Yes, sir," she said. "He's the one."

And the name clicked at once: the man the U.S. sought to support to take over the throne, the man who refused all outside assistance.

"How did you find him? He disappeared three days ago."

"He found me in the desert, sir. He was under some kind of attack."

A moment of silence on the other side. "You must

stay with him. It is imperative for the region's stability that he remains alive. As of now, your number-one objective is to ensure that. Your mission just changed, soldier. You're now assigned to his personal protection."

Chapter Three

The camel dung would hit the fan when Saeed found out about this.

"Yes, sir," Dara said, no matter how much she hated the idea. She had the feeling Saeed would have a few words to say about her being his bodyguard. She was a woman, her new role hardly acceptable in his culture. Plus she was an outsider, and he was famous for resisting all cooperation with foreigners.

"I will try to get in touch as soon as I have anything else to report." She clicked off, put the letters and the phone back and closed the briefcase, then turned to sneak back to her bed. Before she made it two steps, she was enfolded in a viselike grip, one arm around her waist holding her hard, a hand over her mouth.

She jammed her elbows back into her attacker, threw her full weight to the floor, hoping to slip from his grip, trying to get him off her back without killing him. Couldn't chance that, considering that most likely "he" was Saeed, not recognizing her in the dark and taking her for some kind of an intruder.

Damn. If he let go of her mouth, she could explain. No such luck. And he was strong. Fighting him off without harming him appeared increasingly difficult.

They tumbled to the carpet together. She could not shake him. His elbow came into hard contact with her ribs, sending a bolt of pain up her side. Fine. The gloves were coming off. She kicked, missing him narrowly, her feet getting caught in the tent flap. It opened a few inches, letting in some moonlight.

They rolled. She kicked again, hit flesh this time. The narrow shaft of light fell on the man's head. His face was wrapped in a black headdress that showed small, vicious brown eyes glinting with predatory hunger.

She stared into the stranger's gaze, surprised for a split second, then she began to fight in earnest. He was thin but strong. She twisted, kicked with both feet. He rolled back. She jumped up, ready to push her advantage, wishing she was running on full steam. He lurched at her before she could reach him, and sent them both sprawling again.

Damn. This time she landed on her bad shoulder, with his added weight on top of her. Hot pain shot down her arm, and she sucked in her breath, blinked to clear the stars from her eyes. The next second, she felt the blade at her throat.

Then the tent flap flew open and a vision stood outlined in the opening: Saeed, his long white shirt cascading from wide shoulders, the moonlight glinting off the curved dagger in his hand.

The attacker jumped up and charged at him, the two men coming together with a battle cry.

She sprang to her feet. Why was she the only one without a weapon? How the hell was she supposed to protect him?

The men fought, then separated to circle each other, then lunged into a clash again. She watched them, waiting for an opportunity. The attacker staggered back, blood gushing from his arm. He extended his hand as if to drop his knife in capitulation, but in the last split second he threw it instead—with force.

She didn't have time to think. Instinct pushed her forward. She caught a glimpse of surprise on Saeed's face before he propelled himself at her to knock her out of the way, taking her to the ground. He had already thrown his own dagger.

It hit its mark.

She stared at the attacker's limp body not ten feet from them, then noticed that Saeed, on top of her, wasn't moving either.

Was he hit? She turned her head to look at him.

His blue eyes stared at her with such intensity she

couldn't breathe. His muscular body pressed into hers. The adrenaline of the fight still pumped through her veins, every nerve ending alive. Having the prince of the desert lying on her did nothing to settle her down. "I—"

Voices filtered in from outside. A dozen or so men poured into the tent with guns drawn. The first few pulled up short, looking from them to the dead man.

After Saeed came to his feet, she sat up, grateful for the air that was slowly returning to her lungs. Any minute now and her brain would start working, too. She hoped.

One of the men said something she didn't understand. Must have been a joke, because the rest of them laughed.

Saeed talked to them in Arabic, and they quieted. One of them responded before they backed out, taking the body with them.

"We will talk. Now." He closed the flap before he stepped to her and extended a hand to help her up.

She ignored it and stood on her own.

He lit a lamp.

Oops. She stepped forward. She'd been lying in his bed. *They'd* been lying in his bed.

He flooded her senses. And he wasn't doing anything, just standing there, looking at her. She had to get a grip. He wasn't the first handsome man she'd come across. In the SDDU, men outnumbered women twenty to one, all of them well-built, powerful, in their prime. But none of them had ever unnerved her the way this one did.

And she couldn't put it down to adrenaline. Not all of it.

She had experienced attraction at first sight before, but never this strong, and her rational mind had usually talked her out of it. At the moment, her rational mind wasn't functioning.

He was a hairbreadth from her. She didn't recall either of them moving.

He touched his lips to hers and she fell into his kiss. Plummeted.

And it was like silk, and honey, and going home. Familiar, as if she'd known him before and they had kissed like this, perhaps in a dream that she had long forgotten.

The tent disappeared from around them, and the desert, and their countries. They had no separate identities, but a man and a woman joined together as one, floating under the stars.

And after an eternity, she felt a nudge of conscience and drew away.

"Don't do that again," she said, realizing her protest was too weak and too late. She hadn't exactly kicked and screamed when the prince of the desert had had her in a lip lock.

It helped that he looked as stunned as she felt.

Took a little off the edge of her anger, though not enough to let it go.

"Just because you saved my life, it doesn't mean that you can take liberties with my body." Better make that clear now if they were to work together.

He inclined his head. "I apologize."

"I do, too." The bluster went out of her all of a sudden. She was here to do a job. What she had just done fell miles outside the borders of professional conduct.

Better focus on the task ahead. She drew her spine straight and tall.

"I haven't been completely honest before. My name is Dara Alexander. I work for the United States government. My orders are to protect you."

His face hardened as he stepped back. "Absolutely not."

SAEED SWALLOWED HIS ANGER, damning his rising lust that proved to be harder to control. So she was military. He wasn't surprised. Her camouflage uniform; her skill with the knife; the efficient, in control way she moved supported her claim. "You don't have a dog tag."

"I'm in a special unit."

"And what unit would that be? The kind that engages in unauthorized missions in foreign countries?"

She remained silent, but from the carefully blank look on her face he knew he had hit close. "You must leave."

The woman folded her arms. "I have my orders." Her body language made it clear she had no intention of going anywhere.

As skeptical as he had been about her amnesia, he believed her now. The picture slowly forming in his head fit her.

"You have to leave us," he said again, trying to be patient. "After you recover, of course." She was a guest in his tent and, in the desert, hospitality to strangers was the law of the land. Three days was customary. Required. Even if the man who walked into your camp was your worst enemy. A Bedu breaking the custom would have brought shame to his family for generations. A sheik who did not offer hospitality brought shame to his whole tribe.

"You're welcome in my tent until we leave for Tihrin. Then I'll take you to your people."

She nodded, but he didn't think she was really agreeing. Stubbornness was written all over her beautiful face, apparent in the stiff set of her shoulders. She was buying time.

"In the meanwhile, I'm going to need some weapons," she said with an easy smile, confirming his suspicions.

"You are not my bodyguard. You are my guest." The sooner she accepted that the better.

"No offense, but it looks to me like you aren't exactly Mr. Popularity these days." She gave him a pointed look. "Even if I didn't guard you, I would still need something to protect myself. We've been attacked twice in two days. Sharing your company could be hazardous for my health."

She had a point there. She *had* come into danger because of him. He watched her face for a few moments. "You were attacked in my home. I apologize. It is my duty to protect my guests."

"You'll give me a gun then?"

She was tenacious—a most unbecoming trait in a woman. "No."

"You know, you're a real piece of work. Can I at least have my knives back?"

He watched her eyes, trying to read her true intent. Could she be trusted?

"If any of my people come to harm at your hand, you will answer to me." He reached under one of the pillows and pulled the knives out, handed them to her. "It will matter not that you are a woman."

She nodded.

He hoped she was smart enough to heed his words. "Tell me what you are doing in my country."

"Fighting terrorism."

"And your presence here is authorized by our government?" He waited to see if she would lie. King Majid had turned his back on his foreign allies as soon as they first began to criticize his methods of ruling.

"I'm a soldier. I'm not privy to government nego- tiations. I get an order, I follow it."

"You think I have ties to terrorists?"

She shook her head. "But I think the people who are trying to kill you might."

He had considered that. And as much as he wanted to deny it, he couldn't. Majid was determined to keep power. He would support anyone who supported him, never realizing what harm he might do in the long term.

"So you were dropped in the middle of the desert without food and water to find and protect me?"

"I was on another mission at the time."

"But you got reassigned?"

She nodded.

"How fortunate for me."

"I'm here to help you." She stood, obsidian eyes flashing. "You should be happy."

"I did not ask for help."

"Look, I'm here anyway. Maybe I can help, maybe I can't. What is it going to hurt to let me hang around?"

Plenty, he thought. It would hurt plenty. He could not afford to be distracted now. And he didn't need another person to feel responsible for. He didn't need to be thinking about kissing her again, wanting it so much he had a hard time focusing on anything else, like explaining to her how impossible her long-term presence would be here.

"I'm going to check the perimeter of the camp." She moved toward the tent flap. "I have to start thinking about how to make it more secure, ASAP. Your guys are going to be okay with me walking around, right?"

She was going to secure his camp. The thought was as laughable as exasperating. An affront, really, but he decided not to take offense. He nodded and followed her out, instead of forbidding her to leave. Because he couldn't be sure if they stayed inside he wouldn't again taste her lips. And he wasn't sure if he could stop there.

He shook off the weakness. He could not afford to let her foreign beauty get to him. Not now. Not ever. Not this woman.

She had no place in his life, not on the professional level and certainly not on the personal. She was of a different people. There could never be any understanding between them. He had too many principles to take her as his mistress and to consider her as more was unthinkable. The only choice open to him was to ignore whatever insane attraction existed between them.

DARA STEPPED OUT into the starry night and took a deep breath. The camp looked deceptively peaceful, about fifty tents scattered across the sand, surrounded by a makeshift barbed-wire fence.

"This is your security?" She turned to him. He had to be kidding.

"It keeps the camels from wandering into camp and chewing up everything." He took her by the shoulders and turned her, pointing into the darkness.

He was too close, his touch on her body too distracting. It took a while before she made out the nearly invisible figure of a man among the shadows. She turned her head then to look for more and found them, sitting at irregular intervals, blending into the night.

"That is our security," he said, and withdrew his hand.

"But the attacker slipped through."

"No he didn't. He was one of ours. A servant Nasir hired a few months ago."

"Someone got to him?"

He nodded, his expression grave. "He had a large family to support back home."

She processed that information as she moved forward. "Is there anyone else in camp you don't trust one hundred percent?"

He stepped in front of her and stopped, his gaze searching her face. "You," he said.

"Why?"

"What brings you here?"

"Orders from my superior officer."

"Why would he issue such orders?"

"My government wishes to see your country stable."

"Why?"

"Instability in this region is not a good thing." Truth be told, instability anywhere was bad. The world was getting increasingly smaller; the fate of one nation affected that of many others.

"You are here to ensure I live, so I can take the throne and will be grateful enough to your government to sign an economic treaty."

And she couldn't say anything to that, because it was probably true. She wasn't so naive as to think money didn't come into play when it came to politics.

They walked on in silence for a while. She looked at the camels outside the barbed wire, a herd of penned-in goats, and blinked when she spotted a very modern water truck. The camp was a study in contrast, old and new mixed together. And she couldn't help thinking of the reservation, her grandfather's double-wide trailer with the traditional Lenape tent pitched in the front yard for decoration.

For a moment she felt an infinite closeness to the man next to her and the people sleeping in their tents around them. And her heart ached for what they were, because she knew their world was slowly disappearing.

"Are you satisfied?" Saeed watched her closely.

"Is this the whole tribe?" She scanned the sleeping camp.

He shook his head. "It's our *fakhadh.* The closest of our family. There's not enough grazing to accommodate a whole tribe living together. Our people number in the thousands."

"And you're the boss?"

A small smile played on his lips. "The sheik rules by consensus. It's not as if I can blindly order people around and they'll follow me. When something needs to be done, I consult the elders, the heads of each *fakhadh*. I'm more the father of the tribe than a ruler. Same for the confederation."

She gave him a questioning look.

"Fourteen of the eastern tribes are joined in a confederation. They chose me as their leader."

"Do you live here?"

He shook his head. "I come as often as I can. Nasir stays with the *fakhadh*. Mostly I stay in Tihrin to take care of business. And do some politicking, of course. It's a necessary evil."

She wondered if he liked the modern life of the city, or merely sacrificed his preferences for his people. She imagined his position required an awful lot of sacrifice. In that sense they were similar. Her job, on a much smaller scale than his, had its own restrictions on life. Being part of a top-secret military unit, off on some covert operation most of the time, did not leave time for normal relationships.

She had no friends outside the temporary teams she was put on from time to time. Any relationship with an outsider would have had to be based on lies, and she couldn't stomach that. She could never reveal what she did for a living, where she went when she disappeared for months at a time.

For the most part, she didn't mind being lonely. Life was full of sacrifices no matter who you were or what you did. She glanced at Saeed. Bet he had to give up plenty. But he did have his *fakhadh.* She looked at the tents that surrounded them. His close family consisted of a hundred people. It was mind-boggling for someone like her who had nobody.

Okay, pity party over. Focus on the job. "How about you let me try to protect you as best as I can? You can worry about what treaty you want to sign once you're on the throne."

His voice had a hint of tired resignation in it when he spoke. "I have no intention of taking the throne," he said.

SAEED STARED AT THE DIVIDER, knowing Dara was settling in to sleep on the other side, and felt the weight of his five years of widowhood for the first time. He had loved his wife, although it had not been a love match at the beginning. The marriage had been arranged by one of his uncles. Sheikhah had been a good wife and a good mother.

But he could not recall her drawing his thoughts and eyes as the American woman did. He was grateful for the divider. Whatever his eager body was tell-ing him, she was the wrong woman at the wrong time. But maybe when this was all settled, and Majid's attention was off him, he would seek another wife. Nasir had been singing the praises of the beauty of the daughters of Sheik Amrar long enough.

He tried to imagine for a moment what it would be like to have someone to turn to in the night again, but it was Dara Alexander's face that appeared in his mind.

And in his room.

Saeed sat up as she parted the divider and came in, her blankets tucked under a slender arm. He watched her set them up in front of the entrance flap with graceful movements, not six feet from him.

"What are you doing?"

"Guarding you."

So he had failed to show her reason during their walk. He wasn't surprised. "It is not necessary."

"Humor me." Her hair had been let down, a silk frame to her captivating face.

"I do not want my men to find you here." Surely she would at least be mindful of her honor.

She settled down, the soft light of the camp reflecting in her eyes. "Too late."

He stared at her, hating that she was right. "You are an exceedingly stubborn woman."

She grinned at him. "You'll get used to it."

But he doubted he would ever get used to her at all.

"I've been thinking," she said.

So have I, he thought. But he wasn't about to share his thoughts with her.

"So the king is trying to have you killed?"

Her directness caught him by surprise. He said nothing.

"Does he know you don't want the throne?"

"He should. He is family. I owe him blood allegiance."

"A lot of people wish to see you rule. It must make him nervous."

"Western powers wish to see me rule. They did not see what I saw. My country lost enough men. I will not bring about another civil war."

"Your own people are rising up."

"They forget too soon."

She lay down facing him and pulled the blanket over herself. "You never gave me an answer before. Will you let me protect you?"

And from the stubborn set of her beautiful eyes, he knew it was a rhetorical question. She would try to protect him whether he agreed to it or not. Those were her orders. She just wanted to know if she would have to do it the easy or the hard way.

Still, he owed her the truth. "It's out of the question, Miss Alexander."

"Call me Dara."

"Dara," he said, not altogether comfortable with

it, not comfortable with the presence of the woman in his room at all.

If she were Bedu, he would have to marry her or face her family. "Do you have any brothers?"

"I'm an only child."

"Your father?"

"Gone. I don't have any living male relatives so if you're thinking about trying to call someone to order me home, you'll have to come up with another plan."

She didn't have anyone to protect her. That didn't seem right. A woman as beautiful as she definitely needed protection, whether it was the custom of her people or not.

"People will think you're my mistress," he said, and felt a passing pang of guilt. He had ordered everyone but the servant from his tent to Nasir's, not trusting the stranger with his son and sisters. And his men *had* seen them—in his side of the tent, together.

It took her a long time to come up with a comeback. "I do my job, you stay alive. When I leave, they'll forget all about me."

She was right. The talk she had caused all around the fires tonight would die down in a day or two. Everybody and his brother had a mistress—and sometimes they shared her. Majid had several. Saeed hardly knew anyone in the government who didn't. Majid's nephew flew in high-class prostitutes from Paris on alternating weekends to entertain at his parties.

But it was different with the Bedu. The old code of honor still held out here in the desert. And it mattered to him. He did not want his people to think he had abandoned the honor of his ancestors for the ways of the city.

He reached out and turned off the lamp. After a moment, once his eyes got used to the darkness, he could see the outline of her body in the moonlight that filtered through the loosely woven material of the tent.

She was lying on her side, motionless, guarding the flap.

He didn't want her there.

To be completely honest, he wanted her under him.

He was no better than the men whose loose morals and decadence he'd so often criticized.

He turned his back to her. "Tomorrow we leave for Tihrin," he said, making up his mind. It would be easier to avoid her at the house. Thirty-seven rooms should be plenty enough for her to get lost in.

And with him gone, the camp should be safer.

Even more than the American woman with her bodyguard delusions, the strangers on the hill the day before worried him. They had gone by the time he and his men looped around to surprise them.

And tonight there had been an assassin in his own tent.

He had brought danger to his family. He would

leave his son and sisters in Nasir's protection, have them move farther into the desert. Hopefully he would draw the men who sought to harm him to the city.

KING MAJID LOOKED over the inner courtyard from his office on the top floor of the palace. Soldiers guarded every entrance, their rifle barrels glinting in the moonlight. He turned at the sound of the door opening behind him.

"*Assalamu alaikum.*" Jumaa bowed.

"*Walaikum assalam.*" He returned the greeting, thinking for a moment of the irony of it, wishing peace, when they were here to plan war.

"I trust your journey was not difficult." He motioned the prime minister to the leather couch and sat in his favorite armchair opposite him, his hand resting so the pistol hidden under the pillow was in easy reach. These days he trusted no one, not even the man he had handpicked three years ago then arranged to have elected.

That's why he was still king. His father Abdullah had been too trusting, and his uncle Ahmad before him. And look where it got them.

"Shukrah. With Allah's blessing we were successful," the man said.

Majid nodded as he pointed to the low table laden with food. "Please, help yourself." He poured a half a cup of coffee and handed it to the man, who drank it and handed it back for a refill. They repeated the ritual two more times before Jumaa shook his cup from side to side to signal he had had enough, as custom dictated.

"How much do we have?"

Jurmaa met his eye and said, "Enough to carry out the first part of our plan. Another shipment is coming that should be big enough for the liberation."

Majid nodded, and trusted that eventually the world would see it so, as liberation of lands that had belonged to his ancestors, not as the invasion of northern Yemen. But before that, to ensure the success of that heroic mission, the American Air Force base just on the other side of the Beharrainian-Saudi border had to be taken care of.

He couldn't risk having a U.S. force of any kind that close, a base for the rest the U.S. would send. And they would send troops, he was sure of that. They never could stop themselves from meddling in everybody's business, fancying themselves the policemen of the world.

They viewed all war in this section of the globe as destabilization of the region, a threat to their oil interests. They were scared of what would happen if the oil was finally controlled by the ones to whom it belonged.

He would get to that. First he would get back the lands that were his and restore his country to what it always should have been. Then his neighbors would see his strength and accept him as leader against the foreign enemy.

"Is the army ready?" Jumaa asked.

"They are always ready. And now they have the appropriate weapons."

They needed those, the latest technology, not the hand-me-downs Western powers had provided to support him in ending the civil war, in the hope of fat contracts. They wouldn't sell him weapons now. The relationship had soured. Did they think he would give so much control to them? He had gone to battle to regain the throne of his father and rule as a king was meant to rule, not to be a puppet for the West.

"I worry about the unrest."

He stiffened at Jumaa's bad manners, to bring up something like that. "It's only that. Once the people understand our purpose they will unite behind us." Did he not unite the country after the civil war?

"Of course."

"You are taking care of the source of the recent difficulties as agreed?" He hoped Jumaa had news for him on that.

"We should hear from my men by the end of the day."

Majid nodded. The betrayal angered him. But too many sources confirmed it for it not to be true. He could not look the other way. People under severe torture rarely lied. In the end they all told everything. And they all died with one name on their lips. His cousin's.

He remembered their childhood, the time they'd spent in the desert together as young men, hunting with his uncle's prized falcons and salukis. They had been like brothers back then.

He was going to mourn Saeed when he died.

Chapter Four

Dara scanned the side of the wadi, unease prickling her skin as Saeed drove, his hands relaxed on the steering wheel, his mind—judging from the intense expression on his face—already in Tihrin. She glanced at his rifle between them, opened her mouth to point out again how insane he was to leave her unarmed, then thought better of it. No sense in wasting even that little bit of energy on him. The man was convinced that the eight Bedu he had brought to escort them to Tihrin was more than sufficient protection.

At least she'd been able to talk him into leaving his great-grandfather's hallowed Remington behind for an AK-47. Sheik Saeed was pretty sentimental about certain things. It didn't surprise her. From what she'd seen so far, he was an old-fashioned guy.

She watched the ground in front of them out of habit, knowing it was useless. She was in the second vehicle. If somebody had thought to hide land mines under the rocky, dry river bottom, the first SUV would be the one to get it. She should have warned the driver.

And just as she thought of him, the man beeped the horn in warning. Dara looked up, grabbed for Saeed's rifle, and had only time to point it out the window before the pickups came over the side of the wadi, sending a spray of bullets at the two-car convoy.

She took aim and returned fire. The other three men in the back of their car did the same. Saeed drove with one hand, holding a pistol out the window with the other.

His men in the SUV in front of them were shooting hard, too; looked like all five were still alive. Dara steadied the rifle and squeezed off one shot after the other. They should have brought more men and armed them better. But Saeed had wanted to leave as many fighters behind as he could to secure the camp.

The attackers, plenty of them, rode in four pickups—a half dozen armed men in the back of each. Looked like they weren't taking chances this time. They were trying to surround the two SUVs at the bottom of the wadi like hunting jackals, pursuing their prey.

The wind blew her veil in front of her face and she ripped it off. She had to see, damn it. She aimed systematically at the tires of the two vehicles on her side. It took forever but she hit the two front tires of one. The pickup slowed but kept on coming, rubber slashing, metal throwing sparks on stones.

When it finally stopped, the men jumped off the back and chased them still, guns blazing. She didn't bother with them. They'd be out of firing range soon enough. She aimed at the next pickup, but her hands jerked as her seat got bumped.

She glanced back. The man behind her was slumped forward, blood running down his temple. Damn. She turned from him and took aim again, but she didn't seem to have any luck with the second pickup. Saeed was driving like a madman, the SUV jerking around. He tossed his empty handgun to the floor, held his hand out. She handed him back his rifle, grabbed the one the man behind her had dropped.

She had trouble taking aim, the SUV bouncing too much. She shot at the pickup's front right tire, hit the radiator. The billowing steam made it difficult to see the men behind the windshield. She aimed and squeezed the trigger, but her aim was thrown off again, this time by an explosion.

Damn. She stared at the SUV ahead of them going up in flames, the roof peeled back, not a man alive. One of the attackers had hit the gas tank. Saeed said something in Arabic. He maneuvered around the vehicle deftly, but it slowed him down. The remaining pickups were closing in.

She took aim again, hitting the driver this time. She could see the surprise on his face through the broken windshield. The vehicle slowed.

She turned away from them, took a quick check on the other side. One pickup still going there. From their SUV, only Saeed was firing. She looked back at the three bodies in the back, splattered with blood. They had been in a vulnerable spot, easily picked off through the back window.

Dara watched the men fire from the pickup that was closing the distance on their left. She had to get to the seat behind Saeed, couldn't hit anything from here.

She released her seat belt and climbed back, maneuvering the rifle, yanking her dress that had gotten snagged on the seat. Why the hell had she let herself be talked into dressing like a woman? She was here as a bodyguard, damn it. She had to be ready and unencumbered.

She made it to the back and half sat on a dead man's lap, feeling the wetness as his blood soaked through her clothes. She shut out everything but the men firing, took aim and watched as one of them tumbled to the sand from the back of the vehicle.

She squeezed off another shot, tossed the empty rifle out the window, and grabbed another one from the floor.

Pain bit into her left arm, just below the elbow. Blood bloomed on her dress at once. She swore.

"Are you hurt?" Saeed was looking at her in the rearview mirror.

She flexed her fingers. Everything moved. Flesh wound. It bled, but not enough to concern her. "Fine," she said and continued shooting.

She got a tire just as Saeed got the driver. The pickup came to a halt but the men in the back were still firing.

"Get down," Saeed yelled and slid lower in his own seat, focusing on getting them out of firing range as fast as possible.

She did as he asked, pulled the belt off the man next to her, grabbed her veil from the front seat and made a tourniquet for her arm. Any blood loss had a way of weakening the body, and she couldn't afford to be held back now.

Saeed was watching her in the rearview mirror. "I'm going to take a look at you." He slowed the car.

"Don't even think about it. Whatever happens, do not stop." She climbed to the front, held her arm out so he could see with his own eyes that there was nothing to worry about.

"Is it broken?" He didn't look any less worried.

She shook her head. "I'm fine."

He stepped on the gas again, his voice clipped when he spoke. "You should not be here. I shouldn't have brought you."

She wasn't in the mood for any chauvinistic

garbage. "Because women are weak?" she challenged him.

He looked at her for a long moment. "Women should be cherished."

She stared back, unsure what to say to that.

Her father used to say women had to be toughened up to be fit for the military. He hadn't meant it disparagingly. He merely saw the difference between the sexes as a weakness. He was forever frustrated with her mother's inability to hold up under pressure, suck it up and stick it out.

She glanced at Saeed. *Cherished.* It fell so far outside the realm of her experience, she couldn't even picture it. Was he for real?

They drove on in silence for a while, Saeed focusing on the road while she mulled over the attack.

"How did they know we were coming?"

He shrugged. "They were probably watching the camp."

"You could have sent men out to take care of that." His carelessness surprised her.

"I wanted them to know I was leaving." His voice was low and rough.

"To keep them away from your son?"

"From all my people." He shook his head. "I thought I could protect you."

"You did."

"I expected a sole assassin. Or at worst, two or

three working together." His mouth was set in a thin line, his expression dark. "I was ill-prepared and my guards have died for it. Only by the grace of Allah you're alive."

She would have liked to think her shooting skills had something to do with that, too, but it didn't seem like the right time to argue with him. He looked to be in a bad enough mood already.

"If you agreed to work together with the U.S. government, your difficulties could be solved twice as fast and you could be back with Salah," she said.

He turned his intense blue eyes to her. "Do not," he said, his voice cold now, "use my son to try to manipulate me."

"I'm sorry." And she was. He obviously cared deeply for the boy.

"He'll be safe with Nasir," he said, but she could hear the worry in his voice.

"I'm sure the tribe would give their lives for him."

He nodded. "They would."

"He looks a lot like you."

He took a slow breath and his shoulders relaxed a little. "He's a brave little man. He learned to ride a camel when he was three."

His deep fatherly love and pride, evident on his face and in his words, tugged at her heart. Snap out of it. She turned from him to scan the desert. She was here to guard the sheik, not to fall under his charm.

"IS ANYTHING WRONG?"

"I didn't expect a palace." Dara eyed the marble floor and the priceless artwork on the walls, as Saeed gave orders to the servants.

"My father was once king," he said to her when he was done with them.

"He sure was." She stared at an ornately decorated golden bowl, the size of her kitchen sink back home, displayed on a carved pedestal.

And all of a sudden she felt a wide schism open between them. In the car, during the gunfight, for a few brief moments they were partners, teammates. There was nothing like walking into his palace to drive home the point that someday very soon he would be king. And she'd be... She'd be on the first flight to wherever the Colonel was sending her next.

"This way." He showed her down the hall, walking tall and comfortable, barely sparing a glance for their surroundings while she gawked. *He* belonged here.

"The doctor will arrive shortly. The servants will help you clean up." He stopped and waited for her to catch up with him.

Naturally. The servants. Who else? She wondered what "help you clean up" meant. Was somebody going to come to wash behind her ears? That'd be interesting.

She was used to lack of privacy in her line of

work. It was a fact of life for women in the military—her shyness had worn off long ago. Whatever they would dish out for her she could take it. She was determined to follow the customs and blend in. She had to gain not only his cooperation but the entire household's if she was to guard him successfully.

They passed through a gorgeous gilded archway, more artwork gracing the hall on the other side. The palace was a far cry from the military housing where she had grown up. Where the hell was he taking her anyway? And then it occurred to her. She stopped. She was willing to follow his country's customs, but only to a point.

"To do my job effectively I need to be near you. I'm not going to…" She hesitated to say the word.

He raised a black eyebrow and waited.

"I will not be stashed away in some harem," she said with righteous indignation. "This is the twenty-first century, for heaven's sake."

A slow grin split his face, his blue eyes sparkling with mirth.

"Would that be a general dislike of harems or just mine?" His voice was way too smooth.

He was toying with her. She threw him a look that would have made veteran commando fighters back down.

It didn't faze him at all. "I don't suppose I could change your mind?"

Oh yeah, he probably thought he was good at the harem thing. She looked away. He probably was.

"Go pester your wives," she said. "I'm here to do a job."

"My wife has been dead for five years." The smile slid off his face. "I never really had a harem. Sorry to disappoint."

God, she was an idiot. Of course, he didn't have a wife. That's why his sisters were taking care of his son. She thought of her own childhood for a moment, her mother coming and going then leaving for good when she was twelve. She was glad Salah had his aunts.

"I'm sorry."

His gaze was steady on her face. "Your apology is not necessary."

But the light mood disappeared from between them. She wanted to say something to make up for her ill-spoken words, but for once, couldn't come up with anything. What did she know about loving and losing? Nothing. She had never allowed herself to risk falling in love.

When he moved forward, she followed him to a door made of hammered copper, bit her lip to keep from gasping when he opened it.

If it wasn't a harem, she didn't know what was.

The room had the look of a luxury spa, unreal in its sumptuousness like a movie set. Her two-bedroom condo in Baltimore, the place she called home in between assignments, was at least a couple of hundred square feet smaller.

Tiled columns reached to the fifteen-foot or so tall ceiling that was painted with a small geometric pattern in teal and gold. She gaped at the two separate sitting areas, one with an entertainment center, one surrounded by books—a corner library.

The canopy bed in the back was freckled with jewel-toned pillows, the carpet it stood on having the look of a priceless antique. Enough open space stretched between the sleeping and living areas to hold a dance party. Through an archway she could see into a smaller room, every surface tiled, a round pool sunk into the floor, a good ten feet in diameter.

The place was overwhelming. She lifted a hand to rub her temple, then winced at the pain in her arm. Fresh blood stained her sleeve.

She heard his sharp intake of breath. The next thing she knew, she was in his arms and they were on their way to the bed.

"You said it was a minor injury," he said in a tight voice as he laid her gently on the brocade cover, a thunderstorm brewing in his eyes.

"It is, I've—"

He hooked two long fingers into the hole the bullet had ripped and tore the material open. Her breath caught in her throat.

Somebody was knocking on the door. When Saeed called out, two women came in. He sent them away.

"Lie down," he said, his face hard set.

"There's nothing wrong with me."

She wasn't used to seeing him off balance. He had kept his cool during the fight, both at the oasis and in the wadi, fought off the assassin in the tent without breaking a sweat. She was starting to get the idea that he'd had considerable practice at skirmishes.

And yet, the sight of a single injured woman rattled him. Not that strange, she thought after a moment. In his culture, men were supposed to keep women protected.

"I'm okay. It wasn't your fault," she said.

"Fine. At least don't move." He went off to the bathroom and came back with a wet towel, dabbed off the dried blood from her skin.

The wound wasn't terribly bad, barely oozing now. She didn't see what the big deal was. "I thought the servants were going to help me clean up."

"I changed my mind. You're not well enough to clean up. We wait for the doctor."

Too bad. Her gaze skipped to the bathroom and she nearly moaned aloud at the thought of sinking chin deep into bubbles. She'd had few luxuries in her life. The tub in the other room was calling her name.

"When I ask you a question, I expect you to tell me the truth." He was still looking at the torn flesh, his eyes dark with disapproval.

"I did. It's nothing. Believe me, I've been in worse shape." And that was the truth.

His hand moved higher on her arm, his thumb skimming over an old bullet wound two to three inches below her shoulder. Pleasure skittered across her skin and she bit her lower lip to make it go away. It didn't quite work. He hesitated on the spot, making a circle around it before running his fingers back to her current injury.

"It's a hell of a lot more than nothing."

She stared at him surprised. First time she had heard him swear. So far he had been cool and collected and regal and all that. And to be truthful, she found it appealing in a strange kind of way. Maybe because he was so different from her. She'd grown up around military men, talking trash, wearing bravado as a uniform, everybody vying for the position of biggest badass on the team.

She found Saeed's elegant restraint attractive. More so because she knew from experience the wall of strength behind it.

He drew a thumb over the bump in her skin below the old scar. "What's this?"

She looked away, hesitated. "Birth-control implant." Not that it was any of his business. She'd thought of having it removed—heaven knew she hadn't needed it in a long time—but never got around to it.

He opened his mouth to say something, but was interrupted by a knock on the door that brought a short gentleman in his fifties, fashionably graying at the temples. The doctor. The man wore a three-piece suit as if he were going to a formal reception. After greeting Saeed, he sat on the bed next to Dara and took her pulse while he looked at the wound, then he pulled a handful of supplies from his bag, all sealed in white paper.

"Don't you have something else to do?" she asked Saeed.

He threw her a hard look, but did not reply.

She didn't know what to make of him. She didn't expect him to be this upset over her injury. Hell, she wasn't. Nobody ever had been. Her mother had always been too seeped in her own misery to notice if anything was wrong with her daughter, and then she had left. Her father's standard response to blood, even when she was a child, had been "Shrug it off, soldier."

The doctor unwrapped a syringe, filled it up and numbed the skin around the wound, before getting out his suturing tools.

Saeed sat on the bed next to her, leaving a proper distance between them. "I'm sorry. You are my guest. As your host I am responsible for your safety."

She looked at him out of the corner of her eye. She was doing her job. Injuries were par for the course. She was his bodyguard. He still didn't get that at all. She shook her head.

Long learning curve ahead.

SHE WAS HURT. The idea pained him. Saeed tapped his fingers on his desk, distracted from the calls he had to make. He found it hard to concentrate with the foreign woman in the house. And he had never needed a clear head more than at the moment. His life depended on it.

He picked up the receiver. The minister of agriculture, he decided. He had already set up a meeting for the next day with the minister of trade. A safe bet, he hoped. He was one of the old guard. Saeed hoped Jumaa hadn't found a way to get to the man yet. If the minister of trade had turned, he could be walking into a trap.

He was dialing the last number when he saw one of his servants approach.

"Yes?" He listened to the phone ring on the other side.

"She is awake, sir."

He nodded his thanks and dismissal as he set down the phone.

The smartest thing he could do would be to stay away from her. It angered him that he couldn't. He wasn't some overeager schoolboy. He was a man with a man's control. Except when it came to her.

He'd been lost from the moment he'd kissed her. No, he corrected after a moment of reflection. He'd been lost since long before that—since he'd first looked into her gold-speckled ebony eyes.

He wanted her. He wanted her despite her stubbornness, despite her unreasonable nature, despite the fact that they were as unsuitable for each other as two people ever could be. He wanted to write the attraction down to the fact that she was different, a novelty. But he'd seen plenty and even dated some Western women. He'd spent three years in college at Cambridge, and now traveled the world on business frequently.

He walked out of his office, down the halls, then hesitated at her door before opening it. His eyes locked onto her immediately, registering in his peripheral vision one of the maids who was clearing away a tray. He had ordered her dinner to be served in here.

"Almost ready," she said, sitting on the bed, braiding her hair, her slim fingers slipping through the silky strands gracefully, with practiced ease.

He wanted to see it down, to run his own fingers through it. He frowned, not liking the train of thought, then his gaze fell on the camouflage uniform she had put back on.

"It is our custom for women to wear dresses."

She gave him a polite smile, which drew his attention to her full lips. They were pomegranate-red. From the moment he'd seen them, he had thirsted for them.

"Maybe I'll change when we go out," she said, securing the end of her braid with a band.

He was used to having his words taken as direct order and followed. She alone resisted him. He wanted her all the more for it.

"I'm more comfortable in these and there's no one to worry about here in the house. I assume your staff won't report me to the religious police for breaking some code and corrupting morals. They can be trusted?"

"Naturally." He didn't worry about his staff. The only one he didn't trust around her was himself.

"Did you sleep well?" The blood loss and the painkillers the doctor had given her had made her sleepy. It had taken all his powers of persuasion to convince her to take a brief rest. She did so only when he had promised under no circumstances to leave his office while she was not there to protect him.

She nodded as she stood. "Okay, let's go. We can't afford to waste any more time."

He had never known anyone like her. Her single-mindedness was extraordinary. "Where would you like to go?"

"I want to inspect the premises. I have to ascertain they are as secure as they can be made."

He watched her face, marveled at the businesslike tone of her voice. She was still under the illusion that she was his bodyguard.

"My security is excellent, but if you'd like I would be happy to show you around." He was more than willing to spend time in her company.

She passed by him as she stepped out the door, and he let his gaze glide over her—the way the uniform stretched across her breasts, her derriere and slender legs. The belt brought his gaze to the gentle movement of her hips. He swallowed, feeling like a pervert. If he was, she brought it out in him. She made him feel things he hadn't felt since he was a teenager.

He made a point of walking next to her, showed her the living quarters first, then the garden, the roses that had been his father's pride, but it wasn't enough. She wanted to see everything: the kitchen, servants' quarters, the garages. Night had fallen by the time they were done. He ended the tour at the door of his private suite.

"What's this?"

"My rooms."

"I need to see everything."

Naturally. He opened the double doors for her, aware that the only woman to have ever walked through them with him before had been his wife.

She checked his sitting room with military thoroughness, and his office, but hesitated when she stepped into his bedroom, then got over whatever was holding her back and went to it.

"Satisfied?" He stood in the doorway watching her, an unbidden sensation stirring then settling into his guts at the sight of her standing next to his bed.

"Mmm," she responded, distracted.

She was plotting to save him. He could see the wheels turning in her head, and couldn't help a smile at the thought. "Let me escort you back to your room. If you need anything you need only to ask the servants."

He wouldn't have minded spending time with her, a lot more time, but she needed rest. He had found her in the desert near death, only two days before. Food and water had done wonders, but her body had not yet fully recovered. He worried that her new injury might set her back, although the doctor had assured him the wound was superficial.

She walked out of the bedroom, her gaze settling on the black leather couch in his office. "I'll be sleeping here."

"No," he replied on reflex.

She plopped down and gave him a dazzling smile. He didn't suppose any man could resist her when she looked like that.

She bounced on the seat cushions, and her smile widened. "You know, this is not half-bad. Pretty luxurious actually, compared to a couple of places I had to bunk at the last few years." She ran her slim fingers over the fine-grade leather.

And in his head he could see the two of them on that couch. Naked. He swallowed. "Fine. Suit yourself."

Her smile widened. "Once you get used to me, you'll barely even notice I'm here."

He doubted that could ever happen.

He stood there looking at her, hesitated, and considered for a moment asking her to share his bedroom. Pure insanity. He tossed the thought aside. She was injured. He was a civilized man, not an animal.

"Good night." He turned on his heels and retreated, for the first time in his life.

He could hear her "good night" through the closed door as he walked to the middle of the room and stopped, wanting very much to go back to her.

Nothing but madness. He stripped out of his clothes and went into the bathroom, took a long shower, as cold as he could stand it. When he was done, he slipped on silk pajama bottoms and lay on the bed, eyes fixed on the ceiling. No chance of an assassin surprising him in his sleep while she was in the house. Not because she was guarding him, but because he was unlikely to sleep as long as she was near.

He didn't even try not to think about her.

The first hour passed without sleep touching him,

then the second. Then the sound of screaming and clatter in his office ripped open the silence of the night. He was on his feet and through the door in a split second.

Saeed flipped on the light and stopped in his tracks at the sight before him.

Dara was sitting on the chest of one of the maids, Leila, his pistol in her hands, aimed at the whimpering woman's head.

"Let her go," he said, slowly, distinctly.

She stood up, keeping the gun aimed. "She sneaked in here in the dark."

"What happened?" he asked the near hysterical woman in Arabic as he stepped to Dara and held his hand out for the pistol.

She wasn't giving it up. Fine, he'd deal with her later. He was going to have to remember to lock up anything she might use for a weapon. He had a fine staff; he wasn't ashamed to admit that he was attached to them. Some of them had been in service since his father's time. He had considered them more as family members than hired help.

Leila sat up and apologized, on the brink of crying. Her cat had run out when she'd got up to go to the bathroom; she was just looking for the animal.

He translated for Dara, relieved when she finally lowered the gun.

The maid apologized again and when he assured

her he was not angry about the disturbance, she retreated from the room.

"I will not have anyone in my house mistreated," he said, holding Dara's gaze, knowing that the clamoring in his chest wasn't from concern for his staff, although he didn't like anyone in his employ being tackled.

He was having a near heart attack because for a moment he had thought an assassin had gotten in and harmed the woman who had so captivated him, whose safekeeping was his responsibility.

"Did you pull out any of your stitches?" He reached for her arm.

"I don't think so."

"I would like to see."

She shrugged and unbuttoned her shirt, and his throat went dry when he realized she was going to undress. The bandage was too big to roll the sleeve up over it.

She slipped her injured arm out, her shirt hanging off her right shoulder. He tried to look away from her perfect breasts, covered only by a thin cotton camisole that was plain and utilitarian. It drove him mad.

He lifted the bandages then stuck them back on when he was satisfied that she was all right, but he did not let go of her. He pulled her into the bedroom, closed the door behind them.

"I want you to stay here." For more than one reason, he thought, but for now he would settle for her safety.

She must have read him because he saw the fight rise in her eyes. Then the bodyguard in her won and she nodded. She was so serious, ready to perform her duty at all times and under all circumstances. He admired her dedication.

Under her beauty lay a steel core he found irresistible.

He hadn't meant to kiss her, he had merely wanted to protect her, even knowing she was more than capable of looking after herself. But no matter how good his security, nothing was impossible for a man with determination. Or for a woman—he was beginning to believe. If an assassin got in... And at that point of the thought process, reason flew out the window.

Once his gaze fastened on her lips, his head dipped on its own.

She met him halfway. The small gesture made his blood sing.

Chapter Five

Bad idea, Dara thought, even as their lips met. Tingling energy hummed through her system, ran into her limbs.

The kiss was...inevitable.

Something about him overrode her security precautions with ridiculous ease. She sighed and let go. She was a soldier; she recognized the point when fighting became futile.

Her hands crept up his naked torso, and she could feel the play of muscles under her fingertips as he folded his arms around her. Her heartbeat had not yet slowed from the rush of waking up to an intruder, and when Saeed had barged out in nothing but black silk, the settings in her brain had switched from Danger to Lust in an instant. She would have handled danger better, was more prepared for it.

His lips were soft on hers but insistent. The man didn't have a tentative bone in his drool-inducing body. He slipped off the rest of her shirt and pulled her closer, nothing between her nipples and his chest but the thin fabric of her camisole.

He nipped her lower lip, and she opened for him. Then his fingers glided over her ribcage, and his palms covered her breasts. She moaned into his mouth.

He was careful with her, but not hesitant—took everything he wanted. She gave it and wanted to give more, surprised by the strength of her body's response.

In her line of work she was used to being surrounded by guys, them coming on to her in jest or in earnest. She brushed them off on principle. Military missions always required full concentration, and the short breaks she had in between assignments she preferred to spend alone. She was thirty-one and she could count the number of relationships she'd had on one hand with fingers left over.

And if she'd ever had good reason to say no to a man, it was now. But she didn't protest when he picked her up and carried her to the bed, or when he laid her on the coverlet and stretched out next to her.

He looked at her for a long moment, his fingers reaching for the hem of her camisole and sneaking under it. The heat of his touch on her bare skin made her shiver in pleasure. He moved higher and rubbed his thumb over a nipple. She arched into his touch.

He watched her eyes, and she knew he could see the naked shameless need in them. She didn't care.

She ran her hands over soft silk and felt his hardness beneath. And she wanted it. He flexed against her palm. She wanted to feel him flexing inside her. Heat pooled between her legs at the thought.

Something poked against her back, nudged her conscience. She reached to push it away, and her fingers closed around the barrel of the gun. She'd still had the pistol with her when he'd carried her to the bed.

He unbuttoned her pants and slipped his long fingers inside, and she wanted to melt into the sensation, but the cold metal under her own fingers brought back reason.

"No," she said, half-surprised she could still say it, hating to stop him, knowing she must.

He drew back, took a slow breath, closed his eyes. Some of their heat was gone by the time he opened them again.

"You're right," he said. "Not yet. You need to recover." He gathered her against him, his arms a protective circle around her. "Go to sleep," he whispered into her hair.

"YOU SHOULD NOT HAVE COME here," the minister of trade said, his round face pale with sadness and resignation.

"I must do something." Saeed leaned forward in his chair. "I would give my life for our country without hesitation, for our people. But I will not have it taken from me out of paranoia and political madness. I have called some others on the council this morning."

"I know." The man nodded, looking years older than when Saeed had last seen him a few months ago, his hair nearly all white, deep brackets framing his mouth. "You shouldn't have come back to the city."

Anger rose in Saeed swiftly. "I will not cower. Had I stayed, I would have drawn more assassins to my family. I must face my enemies."

"I have heard the people are gathering. A small army…"

"Not my doing." He shot out of the chair. "I swear I do not seek to topple the throne."

"You look very much like your great-grandfather," the minister said after a moment of silence. "I suppose you hear that a lot."

"I believe in peace. It is what we need." He watched the older man. Bringing his great-grandfather into the conversation was no happenstance.

Sheik Zayed was a legendary leader. He had pushed foreigners out of the country and unified the tribes. He had made Beharrain what it was today. Saeed remembered well the man from his childhood, stalwart and full of fire.

After his death, his son Salim had ruled for twenty-nine years before a stroke had forced him to give up the responsibility of ruling to Saeed's father,

Ahmad. But King Ahmad had died before long in an accident, and Saeed's uncle, Abdullah, a man as paranoid as he was weak, had come to the throne. Then came the horrible years of civil war, ended by the iron fist of Abdullah's eldest son, Majib.

Saeed watched the man in front of him, wondering if he could still be trusted. If he, like everyone else since his father's death, expected Saeed to take back the throne eventually.

"We live in delicate times," the man said. "Perhaps a trip abroad for a while."

"I will not run."

"You cannot win a trial if your enemy is the judge."

The man was right, of course. Saeed nodded. And yet he had to do something. He could not run for the rest of his life. "If we could get a group of us together and sit Majid down, break the hold Jumaa has on him. I'm certain he could be made to see what bad counsel he's been getting from the prime minister."

"What goes on at the royal palace is out of our influence. We must stay out of it. If I lose my office, I can be of no use to the people."

Saeed looked at him and read the fear in his eyes. "If we stand together—"

The man shook his head. "It is not widely known, but the king ordered the execution of all political prisoners a week from today. The unrest in the country worries him."

Saeed stared at the minister. Hundreds of men were held in Majid's prisons, some of them Saeed's relatives. At the beginning of his rule, Majid had removed everyone from government about whom he had the slightest suspicion of not supporting him, everyone who raised his voice on any issue against Majid, everyone who questioned whether the succession of the throne should go back to King Ahmad's line.

The political prisoners were a sore subject between Saeed and Majid, one often discussed. Saeed thought they had made progress. He had hoped he could talk his cousin into letting the prisoners go.

He stood to leave, accepting that he would not find the support he sought from the minister of trade, understanding that matters might be even worse than he had thought.

"Ma'al salama," the minister said his goodbye, then added on a quieter voice as Saeed was closing the door behind him, "Allah be merciful."

Saeed walked down the hall, down the stairs, out of the newly renovated offices. But instead of going to his car, he marched straight across the road to King Majid's ostentatious palace. The many-towered building looked like a cross between a grand mosque and the Taj Mahal. But looks could be deceptive. While it looked the picture of dignified civility on top, torture chambers hid below.

There had been a brief time after the civil war

when Majid and he were still friends. Saeed had come and gone from the palace almost daily then, obliging his cousin's request for help with convincing the Bedu sheiks to support the new king. Then he saw too much of the tools his cousin used to preserve the hard-won peace and lost the taste for politics.

He walked up to the gilded gate and noted the extra security. He did not have to identify himself to the guard. "I wish to see my cousin."

The man bowed and allowed him through. He walked across the paved courtyard to the east wing that held the offices, leaving his small handgun with the second set of guards who stood at the doors of the main building.

Climbing two flights of curving marble stairs took him to the red velvet reception room where he was greeted according to his title.

"I apologize, Sheik, I lost your appointment." A nervous little man he had not seen before shuffled his books.

"I do not have an appointment. Is my cousin in the palace today?"

"Please allow me to inquire." He hurried off and returned not five minutes later. "The king is over-joyed at your visit and will see you at once." He snapped his fingers at one of the many clerks who sat at tables behind him, and one came to his feet.

Saeed followed the man through a labyrinth of

corridors to one of King Majid's smaller sitting rooms, one he reserved for private enjoyment.

Majid sat behind an enormous marble-topped desk, cigar in one hand, a tumbler of cognac in the other.

"Assalamu alaikum." Saeed bowed.

"Walaikum assalam, Cousin. I hope you and your family are well and everyone prospers."

"Yes, thank you. May I offer my congratulations on the fortuitous birth of your new prince."

The boy was Majid's twelfth son. The king inclined his head with a small smile, very different from the reaction he'd given at the birth of the first— a full week of fireworks and money distributed on the streets. Clearly the excitement of fatherhood had worn off over the years. "Would you like a drink?"

Saeed watched as the man sipped, breaking the Islamic law of which he was supposed to be the country's supreme defender.

"No, thank you." He sat, thinking his next words over carefully. He had to convince Majid that he was not a threat to the throne.

But the king spoke before Saeed had a chance to make his case.

"I had disturbing news of you lately, Cousin."

"I assure you it is false. My loyalty is to my king and country."

"And yet armies gather and your name is on the rebels' lips."

"I have nothing to do with it, I swear to you." He spoke his words with force and clarity. "You must trust the blood of your family. The prime minister perhaps wishes us not to trust each other for his own purposes. Perhaps Jumaa likes the taste of power too much."

"I am king of this country." Majid's voice rose. "I am not controlled by the prime minister. I assure you, it is quite the other way around. It is bad enough your father allowed the glory of our monarchy to be reduced to a constitutional monarchy. He was a weak man. But I am strong enough to rule as a king was meant to."

Saeed swallowed his anger. His father had been ten times the king Majid was. His father had ruled in the best interest of the people. He looked at Majid and finally understood how wrong he had been about his cousin. And it pained him a great deal because he did not want to go against his own family. But like his father, he also had the interest of the people at heart. And for the sake of the people, he would do anything that had to be done.

The king swirled his drink for a few moments before he talked. "You've disappeared from the city suddenly. You could not be found."

"To defend my life and for no other reason." Saeed watched the man closely as he spoke. "I heard of the upcoming executions. You must reconsider."

"You come to my palace armed, and plead the

case of my enemies," Majid said, the friendliness gone from his voice, his tone hard and cold. "I understand the guard took a weapon from you."

"I gave it over myself. There had been attempts on my life. I must be armed as a precaution."

"Attempts on your life or so you say."

And he heard it in Majid's voice. His fate was decided. It had been decided before he had ever come here. Nasir had been right about their cousin.

"It pains me," the king said as he pushed a button on his phone, "to find that my own family betrays me."

A side door opened and guards poured in, eight of them.

Saeed stood with dignity. "Indeed, blood betraying blood is the worst. May Allah blacken the face of any such man."

He did not resist when they led him away, refused to fight like some petty criminal jostling with the street police. He was sheik, leader of his people, great-grandson of Sheik Zayed. He would find a way out, and whatever was needed to save his nation, he would accomplish.

WHERE THE HELL was he? Dara went through the papers on Saeed's desk for the third time, hoping for a clue. Nothing there. His appointment book was blank for the day.

He'd already been in his office and working when

she'd woken. He had a servant take her to a sumptuous breakfast, indicating he wanted to talk to her
later today. After breakfast, she took a bath in her
guest room. By the time she made her way back to
his office, he was gone. It took her a half hour run-
through of the house to realize he was no longer on
the premises.

The staff would tell her nothing, claiming they
didn't know where he'd gone. And now, midafternoon,
she was really getting worried. She left his desk and
went back to her room, threw an *abaya* over her army
fatigues, veil and head scarf in place to cover her face,
and marched out of the house, straight to the guard at
the gate. They would either tell her where Saeed went
or she would go out on her own and search the streets.

"Where did Saeed go?"

The man looked at her as if she were crazy.
"Please return to house, miss."

"Listen to me—" she began to say, but was cut off
by a loud banging on the gate.

The guard turned from her to slide open the cover
of a small opening to peer outside. He exchanged a
few words with whomever was trying to gain entrance, then opened the door wide and stood aside.

Two dozen or so men poured in, all soldiers. One
of them took the guard's rifle at once. The rest spread
out, disarming men they came in contact with, ignoring the women, issuing orders, entering the house.

"What's going on?" Dara whispered to the guard, not wanting her English to be overheard.

He remained silent for a while before responding. "They had a royal warrant."

She took off for the house, hugging the walls, making sure she looked as scared as the other servant women. She made her way toward Saeed's offices, slinked by and saw the soldiers go through his files, dumping everything on the floor, seizing what they pleased.

They grilled one of the male servants, but she could not understand what they were trying to get out of him. Then one of the soldiers caught her watching, said something to her.

Now what? She stood, rooted to the spot. What did he want? She bowed her head, tried to back away. The man advanced on her, waving his gun. He wasn't big, but he was armed, and she didn't have anything. The pistol she'd taken from Saeed's desk had disappeared by the time she woke that morning.

The soldier yelled at her. She began to tremble, whimper loudly, and covered her face with shaking hands. When the man reached her, she crumbled to the floor sobbing.

He looked at her with contempt, said something in a harsh voice then turned and let her be.

She moved away, half crawling, not standing fully

until she was out of sight. She had to find out what the hell was happening.

She made her way back to the guard at the gate as fast as she could without raising anyone's suspicions. At least he spoke English.

"Somebody must tell Saeed what's going on here. Warn him not to come home. I can do it. I'm a woman, the soldiers are paying no attention to me. I must know where he went."

The guard did not respond.

"Your sheik's life is at stake." She wanted to shake the man, put him in a headlock if she had to, but she couldn't draw attention.

"I do not know where he went," the guard said at last, appearing more upset now. "He did not take a driver."

She went back to the house and questioned any servant she came across, but they would not respond to her. Some, she suspected, because they did not trust a foreigner, others because they did not speak English.

And then, as soon as it began, the invasion was over. Half the soldiers left, carrying boxes of Saeed's papers, the other half remained, guarding all entrances from the street.

She came upon a group of Saeed's guards gathered in the kitchen. They argued. A couple of older servant women wept.

"What happened?" Dara would not let them ignore her.

They looked at her with disapproval, but the guard who'd been at the front gate earlier, Umbarak, answered her. "Sheik Saeed was arrested this morning for treason."

She felt the blood run out of her face. Damn. Keeping the sheik safe was her responsibility. "We must get him at once."

"*Inshallah.* It is now in Allah's hand." The man tried to brush her off.

Anger filled her, anger and worry. "So you'll leave him to his fate?"

"We have sent news to Nasir. It is his place to decide what to do."

"And if it is too late?"

Umbarak looked stricken at the suggestion, but turned from her. He probably thought her rude for speaking out of place. No amount of argument could make him see her point, could make them understand how much danger Saeed was in, could make them accept her as an equal and work with her.

It was painfully frustrating, but she had to accept it and move on to find another solution. She could not change a millennia of tradition in one afternoon. And she didn't have an afternoon. King Majid wanted Saeed dead, and now he had him in his clutches.

"Where would Sheik Saeed be kept?" she asked, ignoring the disapproval of the men.

"There are many prisons in Tihrin, but he would be held at the palace," Umbarak answered.

"Do you not care if he lives or dies?"

Anger flared in the man's eyes. Good. So he did care. She stepped closer, ready to press her advantage.

DARA WALKED AROUND THE PALACE for the third time, noting the position of the guards, the height of the walls, the security cameras. She could have walked around the building a hundred times and not be noticed, thanks to the black *abaya* that made women indistinguishable from each other.

She looked at Umbarak, sitting in the car in the parking lot of a ministry building across the road. He was waiting for her; at last he had finally understood the gravity of the situation. That was something. She turned down a side street, circled the palace again, from farther this time, then again one more street down, then again, in concentric circles, mapping possible escape routes from every exit.

Darkness fell by the time she was satisfied. She walked back toward the palace, noted the locked gate, walked down the street, looking at vehicles until she spotted a truck that was high enough. Popping the lock and hot-wiring took less than three minutes—she'd paid attention during her training.

She drove the short distance to the back of the palace compound where the wall was the lowest, waited for the night patrol to pass by. She had a few minutes before they would loop back again.

She parked the truck as close to the wall as she could, climbed on top and jumped, aiming at the spot where two security cameras stood back to back. She landed exactly between them, out of the range of both. She crouched on the wall and looked around at the flat-roofed building under her, then dropped soundlessly.

She ran across the roof, looked down at the ground, jumped and rolled into the shadow of the building. Garages, she realized, catching a glimpse of a row of luxury cars through the window.

She could see six guards from where she was, all of them relaxed, probably bored, smoking. A servant woman crossed the yard, carrying a small wooden box. Nobody paid her any attention. Dara stood and stepped out of the shadows. The guards looked up for a second before returning to their conversation. She walked toward the same door where she'd seen the woman disappear. Her finger was on the knob when it opened from the inside.

She kept her head down, stepped out of the way of the exiting man hastily. He glanced at her, said something. As if not hearing him, she slipped in the door and kept walking. He stepped back in after her. Damn.

She could not play the woman-scared-into-hysteria here. The royal servants would be used to demands from the royal guard.

He shouted something at her and came closer. She waited until he was no more than two feet away, then she pulled her gun, pointed it at his head with her right hand, put a finger to her lips with the left.

He froze.

"Sheik Saeed." She said the words carefully to make sure he understood her.

He stepped back.

She took the safety off.

He said something on a low voice, stepped closer, and reached for the gun.

The trouble with this country was that nobody believed a woman could be dangerous. And she couldn't even give a warning shot to show him she was. Gunfire would have drawn attention. She rushed him instead, gun to temple, knife to throat, she pressed it just hard enough to draw a little blood. She had his attention now.

"Sheik Saeed," she repeated, satisfied when he pointed down the hallway to the left.

She took the knife from his throat and shoved him in front of her, the pistol in his back. He understood her and moved forward.

Two doors to the left, then a flight of stairs down. She kept track of their approximate location in the building. The corridor down here was narrower, darker. They were coming to a T at the end. She stopped the man, stepped in front of him while keeping her gun trained at his head, peeked around the corner. A row of doors each way, a soldier standing in front of one on her left.

Dara turned around, swung at the man's temple with the butt of the gun, caught him so he wouldn't make too much noise falling to the ground, lowered him slowly.

She tucked his handgun next to hers into her belt under the *abaya* and stepped forward, walked toward the guard without looking at him. He said something, probably ordering her out of the prison. She walked on. He spoke again, his voice angry this time. But she was close enough now. A chop to the man's windpipe dropped him to his knees.

"Keys," she said and pulled her gun, pointed it between his eyes.

He gasped for air, shook his head. Probably didn't even understand her. Too bad for him. She didn't have time to play around. She knocked him out same as the first man, searched his uniform. He didn't have the key. Okay, maybe that was what he had tried to tell her.

She looked the door over, pulled her knife and went to work on the pins in the hinges. Damn, it wasn't easy. She forced the blade into the tiny gap between the top of one pin and the doorjamb, wiggled it. Her efforts were working but too slow. She glanced around—still alone—then wiped her forehead as she focused on the pin again.

When it was out far enough, she popped it free with the butt of her knife and went to work on the second pin. It was even more tightly stuck than the first. *Come on, come on, come on.* She put all she had into it. She hadn't come all this way to fail. She wiggled the pin up with the tip of the knife, wishing she could see through the door, see what shape Saeed was in. She wouldn't allow herself to think that she might not find him alive. He was charged with treason. There must be an official execution. King Majid would want that to legitimize the whole charade. He had to keep Saeed alive for that.

But it didn't mean he hadn't been tortured. She pushed harder, the pin moved up another fraction of an inch, but then the blade slipped and scraped against the door. She didn't worry about the noise, just went back to what she was doing.

If there was someone in the room with Saeed, they would have heard her by now. She was pretty sure he was alone.

The sound of boots scraping the floor came from above her head, people going somewhere on the upper level. She popped the pin, jammed the knife between the door and its frame, put all her weight into it and moved the door enough to get her fingers in the gap, then pulled with all her strength. Damn, that didn't feel good on her bad shoulder.

Saeed sat on a metal bed in a small dingy room, handcuffed to the frame. She took her first deep, real breath since he'd gone missing that morning. Relief rushed blood to her head, drumming through her ears.

"Are you okay?" She leaned the wooden door against the wall to make sure it wouldn't fall and draw attention.

"Dara?"

If she ever saw a man more surprised, she couldn't remember it. Good. Maybe now he would start taking her seriously. "Are you hurt?"

He shook his head.

She handed him the knife before she left to get the guard outside the door. She tied and gagged him before pulling the listless body into the cell, then went and dragged in the other man the same way. He was heavy, made her work up a sweat, starting to come to and fight against his ropes.

Saeed was still trying to open the handcuffs, not easy with his hands bound together. She took the knife from him, tried, and didn't seem to manage any better. Damn. She looked around the room for another tool.

"Your gun," Saeed said.

"They'll hear us."

"Use the pillow."

There was no time to hesitate. "Stand back."

She placed the pillow over the barrel of the gun, pushed it against the chain that held the cuffs together, then squeezed the trigger. The sound echoed through the room, but not as badly as she'd expected, no more than a door slamming shut.

She stripped off her *abaya*, veil and headscarf then tossed them at him. He understood at once and handed her his kaffiyeh from around his neck. She tucked her pistol into her belt, flung the guard's rifle on her shoulder, handed Saeed the extra gun. He hid it under the *abaya* that unfortunately came only to midcalf, and revealed his black suit pants and shoes that obviously belonged to a man. Still, it was the middle of the night. Not many were awake, and she hoped those who were wouldn't be looking too closely.

"We gotta go." She turned, ready to make a run for it, but he caught her by the arm.

"Dara," he said, then crushed her to him and kissed the soul out of her.

And she kissed him back as fiercely as she felt, angry with him for having gone out alone, angry at herself for not knowing better and letting her guard down in more ways than one. And then the anger and fear melted away, and there was nothing but sweet pleasure and the relief that he was alive and she was back in his arms once again.

She smiled when he let her go, and fastened the veil and headscarf in place to cover his face. He gave her a we-will-never-speak-of-this-once-it's-over look, and strode out of the room, pulling her behind him. And it occurred to her how annoyed she used to be when in movies the hero and heroine stopped to come together in a heated kiss in the middle of a chase scene, when every second might mean the difference between life and death. And she wanted to stop him and kiss him again. Because if this was it, if they were going to get nailed on the way out, she wanted to take at least that much with her.

He went up, but in a different direction than she'd come. She followed him, figuring he knew the palace better than she did. Her path of entry wouldn't have worked for a way out anyway. The two of them scaling the garage wall would be bound to draw the guards' attention.

They were in the servants' quarters—small rooms, narrow hallways, not nearly as neat as the rest of the palace. The few who were awake and about paid little attention to the young soldier and the tall woman he escorted.

They reached the door he was apparently looking for. He shot off the lock with a loud bang that raised some shouts behind them. They didn't stick around to see whom they woke, but spilled out into the street.

Straight into the night patrol.

Chapter Six

Saeed heard Dara swear as he blocked her and shot at the men. But if he had hoped she would take the hint and stay safe, he was mistaken. She pushed around him and took out her share of the patrol. The fight was over in seconds.

He ripped the veil and burka from his head as he ran between the bodies out to the street, looking back as much as forward, making sure she was okay.

"You should think about letting me do my job now and then." She caught up with him finally. "Umbarak is on the other side by the east gate. He probably heard the gunfire."

"We don't have time to wait for him."

Few cars were on the street at this hour of the night. He stepped in front of a large luxury sedan and pointed his gun at the driver as more guards poured out of the palace, letting some bullets fly now.

Saeed banged his palm on the hood of the car

when it screeched to a halt in front of him, nearly knocking him over. Then he was at the driver's door, pulling the man out. Dara was already in the passenger seat returning fire by the time he got in. And they were off, flying down the four-lane boulevard named after his legendary great-grandfather, about a dozen royal guards pursuing them.

The good news was that traffic was sparse, making driving easier. The bad news was that the royal guards were shooting as freely as if they were in the middle of the desert, not caring whom or what they hit. And yet he had no choice but to lead them through a densely populated area, the fastest way out of the city.

Dara knelt on her seat, firing back at the guards.

"We cannot harm the people."

She threw him an offended look. "I hit what I aim at."

He turned down a side street, moving away from the highly developed areas and into the outskirts of the city. The farther out they got, the less common streetlights were and the worse the condition of the roads. He wove in and out of a jumble of little alleys, knocking over a jar or a small cart now and then, the turns tight for the car.

A couple of times he got ahead enough so their pursuers were out of sight, but the royal guards were persistent and caught up with them over and over again.

"Hang on," he said the next time they temporarily shook off the men.

He pulled off the road and across a dirt yard, aiming straight at a shack. He drove through the palm-frond side without trouble and stopped, killing the motor.

"Not bad for a sheik, considering you have two chauffeurs."

He saw only the outline of Dara's head in the dark, but could hear the smile in her voice. "You should see me on a camel." He pulled off the *abaya* and tossed it on the back seat.

Sheik Saeed ibn Ahmad ibn Salim had run from his cousin dressed like a woman. He swallowed the humiliation of it. He would not have done so to save his own life. But from the moment Dara had stepped through the cell door, he knew he would do anything to get her out of there alive. Even sacrifice his dignity.

"Don't ever do that again," he said.

"Shoot back at people who are shooting at me? In my line of work, you turn the other cheek, you go home in a body bag."

"Not that," he said, impatient. He was glad she was strong and competent enough to defend herself. He admired her for it. "Don't ever put your life in danger for mine."

"It's my job."

"I refuse protection."

"Because I'm a woman?"

"Because I can take care of myself."

"Me, too," she said, and they both fell silent for a while.

"If things were reversed, if I was arrested for some reason, would you have let me be executed?" she asked.

He hadn't thought he could be more scared for her than he had been for the past hour, but her question turned his blood to ice. She *could* be arrested. She had broken into the palace and freed a prisoner. She could be charged with a pile of offenses, not the least of which was espionage. What she did and did not do wouldn't matter. They would try and hang any charge on her they could.

"Would you?" she asked again on a quiet voice.

He would take the palace apart stone by stone. "No."

"See? Because I'm your guest and according to your customs, you're responsible for me. According to my orders, I'm responsible for you."

He took a deep breath. "You are more than a guest," he said.

She stayed quiet after that.

Cars approached, then moved on. He waited a few minutes, backed out of the shed and took off in the opposite direction, making sure to note the house so he would know where to send reparations later. He didn't slow until they hit the desert and then he had to, the luxury sedan being not exactly designed to race over sand.

Still, he drove as fast as he could. It wouldn't be long before their pursuers figured out where he was heading.

MAJID GRABBED THE EDGE of the table, willing his rage to subside.

"How could it be?"

The captain of the guards would not raise his head to look at him, but remained bowed. "He had help from inside. A servant woman."

A woman? Preposterous. "Search the servants' quarters, find out which one is missing then deal with her family. An example must be made." He would not have traitors in his own palace. "And all who were on guard. For failure of duty. I want them executed in front of the rest."

He watched as the man's skin turned a shade paler, and for a moment considered ordering his execution, as well. After all, he was the captain, responsible for his men.

No. He tossed away the thought. He trusted this one, and trustworthy men were few and far between these days. He couldn't afford to lose any. Too many of those around him, especially in the government, he suspected would favor Saeed.

Saeed. It had always been Saeed. His cousin had been the one their grandfather had groomed for the throne, the man everyone thought golden. Even Ma-

jid's own father, Abduilah, had sworn upon becom-
ing king after his brother's death to rule only until
Saeed came of age.

He pushed that memory away, almost too painful
to bear. He had gotten his uncle, King Ahmad, out of
the way. It had been Majid who had made it possible
for his father to take the throne. And even then Abdullah had favored Saeed. The muscles tightened in
Majid's face. His father had been too soft, unfit to rule.

Majid poured another drink. He, too. had Sheik
Zayed's blood in his veins, stronger than in any of
the great man's other descendants. He always knew
he would sit on the throne some day; although, he
hadn't planned on making his father king first.

But when the opportunity had come to get rid of
Saeed's father, Ahmad, it had been too good to pass
up—the perfect chance to change the line of succession.

They had been on a hunt in the desert and Majid
had gotten separated from the rest with his uncle, the
king. The hawks had been circling, looking for prey.
One of the salukis had scared up something, he
couldn't remember now what it was, and he had
taken aim, racing his hawk to the prey. His uncle had
ridden in front of him and without notice veered into
his path. He had shouted at the man, scared at how
close he had come to shooting the king.

He could recall that moment in detail, the still
that had come over him at the thought, the clarity of

what he had to do. He had aimed again and pulled the trigger.

Afterward he had tied his uncle's body to the saddle and forced his horse into quicksand, then he'd ridden to tell the rest of the hunting party of the terrible accident.

He had never told the truth to anyone, not even his father. Abdullah had been too weak. He would have been shocked to know that it was his son's quick thinking and not the mysterious will of Allah that had put him on the throne. The throne on which he had been ill-equipped to sit. And hadn't he proven it at the end, making one ill-advised decision after the other, allowing the country to slip into civil war. At the beginning, Majid had tried to save him, but at the end he had done whatever he could to hasten his father's demise.

And then with an iron fist, using all the wealth he could raise honestly and by other means, he had created his own army and restored order. The country had accepted his rule without any serious resistance; as Abdullah's son, he was the rightful heir, after all. He had proven that he was fit to sit on the throne by being strong enough to take it.

But now that he had accomplished what he had dreamed of since boyhood, now that the country was his, along came Saeed like a persistent ghost from the past. The people demanded Saeed—the same people Majid had saved from civil war.

It grated on him to have made this one mistake—to have underestimated his cousin. The man had fooled everyone, hadn't he? All his talk of peace and reconciliation, of brotherhood and standing together, and all along he had been planning a rebellion against the rightful king.

"He'd go to his brother." He named the range of dunes where he knew their *fakhadh* would be settled by this time of the year. He had spent enough time there as a child. "He has betrayed me. I wish not to see him alive again."

As soon as the captain of the guards bowed deeper and backed out, Majid reached for the phone.

The country needed a distraction from this rebellion. A common enemy would bring everyone together. The sooner he started the war on Yemen, the sooner the people would realize his vision for the country and would unite behind him.

But first, the U.S. Air Force base across the border had to be destroyed. And then, he would take what was meant to be his.

BY THE TIME THEY GOT within sight of his people's camp, Saeed was vibrating with impatience.

"We have to move fast." He stopped the car at a good distance, stuck his head out the window and called to the guards.

They came over, not lowering their weapons until

they were close enough to recognize him. He greeted the men then drove on, finding not the sleeping camp he had expected, but everyone very much awake.

Tents were coming down, animals herded together, people packing. When he was close enough for them to recognize him, a shout went up with his name, and everyone dropped what they were doing to gather around him.

Nasir, too, came running, hugging him as soon as he stepped out of the car. "You're free."

"A long story. You are moving deeper into the desert?"

"The women and children are—the rest of us were coming to get you. I have sent word to the other tribes."

Saeed glanced around and for the first time, he noticed the men, more heavily armed than usual, weapons piled on the backs of pickups. An impressive feat considering the short time they had had, but still nothing compared to Majid's army.

"I have sent Salah to Saudi with Fatima and Lamis," Nasir said.

He nodded, relieved to hear that his son and sisters were safe. "To Gedad?"

"Yes."

Good. Gedad's house was as safe a place as they came. Their second cousin was a supplier to the U.S. Air Force base just on the other side of the border, his home right next to the base.

"Try to get as many men in the cars as you can, the rest can follow on horseback," Nasir ordered.

Saeed watched the men obey, men for whose lives he was responsible. "We are not ready for a war."

A flash of anger crossed Nasir's face. "Too late. It has already started."

"We haven't the manpower, nor the weapons." But Nasir was right. The war *had* already started. Majid would come after Saeed and anyone who supported him. He would be damned if he would let his people be massacred by his power-hungry cousin. They didn't have much time; they had to prepare. He needed resources.

"I need Hawk."

Nasir looked at him with some surprise, but then said, "I'll help you saddle him." And moved ahead. "There are thirty tribes behind us. We have more than you think," he said too calmly. "Everything is arranged."

How could everything be arranged? How could he have made alliances in such a short time?

And in a moment of understanding, it dawned on Saeed. "You are involved in the rebellion."

His brother smiled, a mixed expression of pride and relief spreading across his face. "I started it."

For a second he was too stunned to comprehend the words, then everything fell into place. Small comments, times when Nasir went here or there on business and then could not be found. But still, bringing together hundreds, thousands of people, had to take enormous coordination, arming them would cost…

"You know of the cave."

Nasir hung his head for a moment before he looked up, passion burning in his eyes. "Forgive me, brother. I could not stand by and watch Majid ruin our country. It boils my blood to see him rule when it should be you." He fell silent for a moment. "Or our father still."

"His death was an accident." They had covered this ground many times before. However misguided Majid was now, bent by the weight of ruling, Saeed had a hard time thinking him capable of murdering his own uncle. Majid had been but a youth at the time, not yet tainted by politics. He remembered their childhood too well, times they spent in the desert, the summers Majid had spent at the palace. He had loved the place.

Loved it too much, maybe?

"He arrested you for treason." Nasir walked next to Saeed with barely controlled fury.

"He felt threatened by the revolt *you* started." No. He'd seen Majid's eyes. He'd known what he was doing. He had planned it. Saeed could no longer make excuses for his cousin. "You're right. We'll do what we must."

They reached the horses at last. He greeted Hawk and grabbed his saddle.

Nasir helped with the bridle. "Where are you going?"

"To the cave. I imagine our assets were seized the moment I was arrested. We need money for better weapons if we're to take the palace."

And it was necessary, even he had to accept it now. The tribes had risen. The fight would not end until either Majid or he was dead. "Wait for me. But not here."

Nasir nodded. "Will you leave the foreign woman with us?"

He hesitated for a moment, looked back to where she was rolling something into a blanket, helping a couple of women. "I'll take her. If I don't, she'll steal a car or a horse and come after me anyway." He did believe that. Dara was nothing if not stubborn.

His brother raised an eyebrow.

"Where will I find you?" Saeed changed the subject to ward off some uncalled for remark on his inability to control a single woman.

"At the old oasis."

"Shelfa?"

The place had been named after the traditional Bedouin spear that it resembled—a long narrow strip of fertile land they rarely used because of the undependability of the weak water source beneath it. Still, for a day or two, it should support the camp. And that was all the time he needed. "*Ma'al salaama,* Brother."

"Alla ysalmak."

He rode Hawk to Dara, watched as she hung food and water on the saddle, and wondered if he was wrong for taking her with him. He should send her to Saudi, to the safety of the American embassy. Of course, she wouldn't go. He could try to talk her into going with Nasir to Shelfa under the relative safety of the camp, but he had a feeling she would refuse that, too.

He held his hand out to help her up behind him, knowing he wasn't doing it because she would demand it, or even because he wanted to keep an eye on her to ensure her safety. He had decided to take her for one reason only—because he wanted her with him.

The admission rocked him. She was the wrong person at the wrong time.

It didn't matter.

THEY RODE THE BETTER PART of the night before they reached their destination, Hawk held back by the weight of two people and their supplies. A car would have been faster and more practical, Dara had thought as they rode, but understood Saeed's wisdom once they walked into the cave. The opening was large enough to allow Hawk in, leaving no telltale sign of their presence that could be seen from outside.

He turned on a flashlight and panned it around. Rocks, rocks and more rocks. She watched as he picked up one from a knee-deep pile in the corner and set it aside. Then another, then another. She went to help him.

"Rest," he said.

"You know, women are not really the weaker sex." She kept on working.

He turned to her and she could see the dark shadow that settled over his face. "They are strong. But still they should be protected."

His voice was hollow, and she got the idea that he was no longer talking about lifting rocks. And the question flew from her lips before she could stop it. "What happened to your wife?"

He went back to working, disassembling the rock pile methodically, stone by stone.

Fine. If he didn't want to talk about it, he didn't have to. But she couldn't help wondering if he had been very much in love with her, if he was in love with her still.

"She was hit by a car," he startled her by saying.

And it sounded so ordinary, as if it were almost unreal. She had expected a scorpion bite or a snake or an overly hard childbirth in the desert without medical help.

"We were in Tihrin. She was shopping for clothes for Salah. She stepped out in front of a speeding car," he went on. "Didn't see it from her burka. They don't allow much peripheral vision."

Didn't she know it. The few times she had to have the thing on drove her crazy. And suddenly she was angry for the death of the woman of whom a moment ago she was jealous. She was angry for Saeed's loss and for Salah's.

"I'm sorry," she said.

He nodded and went back to work.

When he was done, she looked at the exposed slab, about three feet by two. He tried to push it out of the way, but it didn't budge. He sat on the floor, wedged his body against a side wall, pushed with his feet. The large stone moved aside a fraction of an inch.

"If we could move it just a little more we could get a rope behind it and have Hawk pull it," she said as she grabbed on to help.

He nodded and pushed again.

Even with help from the horse, it took over half an hour to move the stone.

Dara peered into the dark narrow shaft open before them. She'd once spent two days in the rat-and-snake infested sewers of Baghdad. She really didn't care to repeat the experience. "You first," she said, and when he crawled forward, she followed him.

After ten yards or so, they came out into an open area, about eight by eight and half as high.

"It's nice down here." She picked up his flashlight and looked around, enjoying the air that stood still instead of swirling with sand. The temperature was comfortable, too.

But he didn't seem to notice it long enough to appreciate it. Saeed ran his hands along the wall, apparently searching for something. Then he found it—a loose rock. He pushed. The rest of the section gave easily, and when she looked closer she realized a small part of the wall wasn't rock after all, but carefully concealed mud brick.

The shaft that opened in front of them was slightly more spacious than the previous one. He grabbed the flashlight and moved forward. They were able to crawl on their knees and elbows, instead of having to slide forward on their bellies.

"This thing has an end, right?" she asked after about fifteen minutes. "I mean you're not planning on hiding out in Beijing, are you?"

"China?" His muffled voice reached her.

What was opposite on the globe from Beharrain? Hawaii? "I mean Honolulu. I feel like we're tunneling straight through."

They came out into another opening, about half the size of the previous one. Saeed sat up and leaned against the wall, set the flashlight aside, and pulled her out of the shaft.

There wasn't all that much room. They were pretty close. "Pink beaches," she said to distract herself, but then the picture of Saeed in a Speedo popped into her mind. Distracting all right, but not exactly what she needed to think about when their knees were touching.

"How about a private beach?" he asked and the slow smile that spread on his face screamed, "Swimwear optional."

"You have one?" She stared at him, dumbstruck both from the idea of owning a private beach in Hawaii and the thought of being there with Saeed.

"My father was king." He laid his hands on the wall again.

The opening they cleared this time was the size of a regular door, and the room behind it too large to be fully lit by the single flashlight they carried.

They stood still while Saeed ran the light over the walls. Wow. The cave before them was as big as a couple of ballrooms put together, the floor littered with jars and rolled up carpets, crates piled high against the walls. Some sort of an ancient warehouse.

"What is this?"

He walked to a hip-high terra-cotta jar, pried the wax seal from its mouth with his dagger and tipped it. Gold coins showered to the ground. "The treasure of my Bedu ancestors," he said.

From time to time she had experienced events in her life that were so far from the expected, so unimaginable, her brain had struggled to accept them, insisting she was dreaming or hallucinating. This was one of them. They were probably dying of exposure somewhere in the desert and she was imagining the comfortable cave and the soft trickle of water....

"Wait a minute—there's water?"

He walked forward, turned a corner behind a larger boulder. She followed him and gasped at the sight. In a side wing of the cave where the ceiling was lower, a steady trickle of water ran over the rocks, collecting into a pool about eight by eleven or so.

From the look on Saeed's face, he didn't expect this, either.

"My grandfather said there was some water down here. I always thought he meant a well."

"You've never been down here before?"

"Never had the need."

She admired his self-restraint while she ogled the pool. After having ridden across a good stretch of desert, acquiring significant amounts of sand in places it didn't belong, the pull of the water was irresistible. She kicked off her shoes, yanked off her socks while hopping on one foot, then finally stuck her toes in. Cool, but not overly so.

He watched her with a smile playing on his lips. "You may bathe if you wish." He set the flashlight on a rock in a way that it illuminated the larger room of the cave but left her in the shadows, then walked away from her.

She shed her clothes and slipped into the pool quickly, held her breath as the cold water surrounded her, swam to the other end then back until she got used to it. Around the edges she could stand up, but in the middle her toes did not touch the bottom.

She dunked her hair in, went under completely and stayed under as long as she could before breaking the surface again, her gaze settling on her dirty clothes. Would have been nice to get them clean.

"Here. Try these."

Saeed's voice made her spin around.

He stood a few feet from the pool's edge, his gaze on her face, and spilled an armload of silk to the ground.

She knew he could not see anything below her neck, there wasn't light enough to see under the water, and yet her pulse quickened, her heart thumping loudly in her chest. She drew a deep breath, trying to relax. It wasn't as if she were shy. Women in the military were not allowed that luxury. She had been on countless missions where she'd been the only female member of the team. She had gotten used to lack of privacy a long time ago.

And yet, Saeed's gaze made her so self-aware she wanted to hide from it, feeling it on her skin as if he had touched her.

"Thank you," she said, hoping he would leave.

He didn't budge.

She stared at him, unable to look away as the light coming from behind illuminated his wide shoulders. Ali Baba and his treasure. The man and everything about him fell way outside her circle of experience.

"I'll be done in a minute and you can take your turn," she said to break the tension between them.

He nodded and turned at last to leave. She watched him as he went back to the crates and looked through them, brought poles and ropes from the back, unrolled a few dozen carpets, made a tent.

She washed her clothes while he secured the top and side flaps, amazed at the elaborateness of the structure that resembled a miniature castle rather than the Bedouin tents she'd seen so far.

She emerged from the water and stayed in the cover of the boulder that separated the pool from the main portion of the cave, pulled the clothes to herself, lifted them one after the other. They weren't clothes after all, but lengths of fabric, silks in every color.

She dried herself in one and wrapped another, pale azure, around her torso. It reached from her armpits to the floor. She took a sea-green piece, folded it in half and twisted it around her waist to make sure nothing gaped open, looped it up to cover her shoulders, but it was long enough only to cover one. Oh, well. She tucked the end into her "waist-band." The end result was a cross between an Indian sari and a woman's toga from ancient Rome. But most of her body was covered and she could be reasonably sure she wouldn't expose herself when she moved. That was what counted.

The silk felt luxurious on her bare skin as she walked toward the tent, wishing for a moment for the kind of style and grace some women were lucky enough to possess, then angry at herself for even thinking of it. She knew little about being alluring, spent most of her life in army fatigues. And it shouldn't have mattered whether Saeed found her attractive or not. It *didn't* matter, she reinforced the thought. Their relationship was strictly professional.

"You look like a water nymph from a myth," he said, looking at her with open admiration.

"A portable palace?" she asked, unsure how to handle the compliment.

"About a tenth of one. I didn't think we needed all of it, but we might as well spend the day in comfort. We can't ride to Shelfa until we have the protection of the night. Too many planes flying overhead." Saeed let his gaze glide over her, sending her heartbeat galloping.

He pulled open one of the front flaps for her. "I suppose in my grandfather's time rulers were more given to pomp and ceremony."

A half dozen oil lamps burned on the sumptuous carpets that covered the floor inside, silk pillows scattered in the corners. The sight took her breath away. A stage set for seduction. She bit her lip to bring herself back to reality.

Saeed wasn't about to seduce her. They were on a mission.

And if he had somehow forgotten that, it was her job to remind him. Still, that he might have thought to seduce her— The idea and the images it brought sent tingles across her skin.

"When I go to the oasis tonight, I wish you would stay here in safety," he said.

And just like that, she was brought back from her little self-indulgent moment of fantasy. He wasn't trying to seduce her, he was trying to get rid of her. She forced herself to be patient. "I couldn't very well guard you from here, could I?"

"You insist on putting yourself in the way of harm." He bit out the words.

"So do you. You went to the palace without taking anyone with you."

"I could have taken every guard I had at the house and it wouldn't have mattered. It would have made Majid's case stronger against me. He would have claimed I went against him with force."

"You could have taken me."

The intense expression on his face broke into a small smile. "You came anyway."

"Exactly. Don't leave me behind again. It takes a

lot of effort to track you down. Effort that would be better spent protecting you."

"I do not need protection."

She gave him an impatient look. Things would go so much smoother if only he were willing to admit that he needed her.

"I would have gotten out of the palace on my own."

"You got out faster with me."

He inclined his head at that, the first sign of agreement he'd shown so far. "I do not want you to come to harm."

"I skirt harm for a living."

"It should not be so," he said, his face serious once again. "A woman like you should be cherished."

She groaned in frustration. "Can you not, even temporarily, consider us partners, working toward a common goal?"

His gaze burned into hers. "Partners in many things but not in fight."

"What the hell does that mean?"

"You must know that you're a very desirable woman."

His deep voice sent tingles to the bottom of her stomach. Then he stepped closer.

Not a good idea. She held out a hand. "Your bath is ready."

He held her gaze for a couple of eternities back-to-back. "I will not rush you," he said, then walked away.

She sank onto a pillow and watched through the open flap as he walked to the edge of the pool, then she squeezed her eyes shut when he began to undress.

Chapter Seven

The water was cold. Good. Saeed leaned his head against the pool's ledge.

The woman was distraction personified. Just what he didn't need right now when everything around him was falling apart. Or perhaps, she was exactly what he needed.

The thought brought his head up.

He didn't like the idea of needing her, liked it even less that the need went beyond the physical. He hadn't expected ever to feel this way about a woman, wasn't sure if it was right.

He threw some water into his face and shook his head. And then he heard her scream. The startled sound bounced off the walls of the cave.

He launched himself out of the pool, wrapped one of the strips of silk around his waist loincloth-style as he ran for the tent. She wasn't there.

"Dara?" Fear filled his lungs. He grabbed his gun,

scanned the cave, blamed himself for leaving her alone. He shouldn't have assumed they were safe for even a moment. Had someone come after them?

"Over here." Her voice sounded muffled.

He followed it, checking behind bigger rocks and stacks of crates.

"I fell through a crack," she said.

And he saw it in a dark corner, an even darker opening in the rock floor. Then he was there and on his stomach, reaching for her.

She grabbed onto his arm. "I didn't see it."

"What the hell were you doing back here?"

"Getting the lay of the land. Looking for an easily defendable spot should anything happen."

He pulled her up, against him, and didn't let go.

"I'm fine," she said, but her voice shook.

He lifted her into his arms, carried her into the tent, and laid her onto the pillows, pulling a lamp closer as he sat to examine her.

No new injuries but a small scrape on the shoulder left exposed by the silk. He waited for his heart to stop trying to jump through his throat.

"Your body looks like a battlefield." His gaze skimmed from the purplish bruise on her right shoulder that peeked from under her makeshift dress, to the bullet wound on her left arm below the elbow, and settled on her latest injuries.

"I'm perfectly fine," she repeated.

Relief untangled his guts at last. "You are."

But he wasn't.

He couldn't stand the thought of anything happening to her, that he might lose her. The thought was akin to physical pain. And reminding himself that she wasn't his only made things worse.

She stood. "I'm going to get some water."

Her movements were graceful and smooth, the creamy skin of her bare arms glowing in the lamplight. Her loose hair, the dark color richer than anything the best painter in the world could mix up, swung forward as she bent to pick through a handful of jars.

He looked at the way the silk fell from her waist over slim legs, at the kissable arc of her slender neck, and knew that a hundred years of looking would not be enough. "I want you."

"Mmm," she murmured, distracted.

"I mean to have you." He gave her fair warning.

She turned, listening now, her eyes as round as the gold coins he had spilled earlier. Her breathing grew shallow. Then she gathered herself.

"What's this?" She lifted a jar in a transparent attempt to distract him.

He broke off the seal and sniffed the contents. "Myrrh and balsam. Both plants have medicinal qualities. Myrrh is thought to help in the healing of wounds." He held her gaze. "Some women rub it into their skin to soften and scent it for their lover. There was a time when it was worth as much as gold."

He dipped a finger into the jar, then captured her left arm and smoothed some ointment over her velvet skin, careful with her injury. He moved up and spread some of the sweet-scented substance over her shoulder, letting his fingers play on her collarbone and the hollow of her neck longer than necessary. He caressed the edges of the fading bruises that peeked from under the silk on her right side.

"That one is fine. It doesn't hurt anymore," she said in a breathless whisper.

Better be sure. He prided himself on being thorough. A quick tug sent the cloth sliding obediently to the ground. She sank to her knees in front of him to retrieve it, bringing them to the same level, but when her fingers closed around the material she didn't get up.

"You are the most beautiful woman I have ever seen," he said, and it scared him to realize that his attraction to her went far beyond beauty. He dipped into the jar again. Some of the ointment, having the consistency of honey, dripped from his fingers before he reached her.

He caressed her soft skin and she swallowed hard, the sound making him smile. He worked the scented substance over her arms, shoulders and neck. When he reached the fabric that covered the rest of her body, he tugged it loose. The silk pooled around her waist.

For a moment he could but stare. Then once his limbs obeyed him again, he dipped into the jar and let his fingers glide over her breasts. She was soft and firm at the same time, the feel of her body starting a thousand burning fires in his. Her glorious breasts glistened in the flickering light of the lamps. She looked like one of the pagan goddesses his people had worshipped centuries ago.

DARA WATCHED HIS EYES DARKEN at her quick intake of breath, as he trailed his fingers from her breasts to her waist and pushed the last of the silk out of the way.

"Lie down," he said, and when she lay on her back, wanting him, ready for him, he surprised her by turning her over.

His hands felt like heaven, melting her bones wherever they roamed. He massaged the myrrh into her shoulder blades, down the curve of her waist, his long fingers caressing her buttocks, dipping between her thighs and pushing them apart. Heat pooled down below. She felt herself grow moist. *Now,* she thought, but he went on to work her legs, the bottom of her feet, covering every inch before he turned her again to take care of the front.

She was mesmerized by his intense blue gaze as he smoothed the scented ointment over her breasts for the second time, dragged his fingers over her belly, her hips, rubbed myrrh onto her inner thighs.

Her skin was so sensitized, each touch sent shivers of pleasure through her. He took his time, and when he was done, when she was a quivering mess beneath his hands, he pulled away.

No. She gathered her strength and came to her knees to face him, wanting to touch his body in turn.

She dipped her own trembling fingers into the jar and let them glide over the muscles of his chest, shocked by the intense pleasure the simple touch brought her.

He came up to his knees, too. Their eyes were level with each other as he pulled her closer, bare skin to bare skin, and claimed her mouth. Her tightened nipples touched his chest at the same time that their lips met, sending a shock of pleasure to her core.

He did not take her mouth gently as he had touched her body, but ravished her lips, made them his in every way. Her heated blood drummed an erratic rhythm as he consumed her, and yet his fervor did not scare her. She reveled in it. He left barely a coherent thought in her mind when he moved back.

"Ya lilly ya aini," he breathed the words.

"What does that mean?"

"You are my eyes," he said with a smile.

"That's beautiful."

"Ya noori. You are my light."

His gaze was on her face, but the burning expression in his eyes and his words touched her as profoundly as if he ran his hands over her body, maybe even more so, leaving not only her skin tingling, but reaching deeper inside.

She leaned forward, into him again, not wanting the sensations to end. She was a grown woman who knew what she wanted, without shyness or apologies. She had seen both the best and the worst life had to offer, too much perhaps of the latter. In her line of work, moments of respite were few and far between. Moments like this... She'd never quite had one like this before.

Saeed held her gaze, took her hand and placed it on the top of the fabric twisted around his waist. She understood his unspoken message: it was up to her how they proceeded. He was willing to stop even now.

She wasn't.

Without hesitation—although, with slightly shaky fingers—she pulled the material free. To see his obvious proof of desire was a heady feeling. Touching it raised her body's level of urgency a notch. She moved to straddle his lap, but he put a hand to her waist and stopped her halfway.

The protest died on her lips when his other hand cupped her, long fingers parting her flesh. He worked her with finesse and patience that took her breath away. When his hot lips closed around her nipple—his teeth grazing the hard tip—she held on to his shoulders and let her head fall back.

He felt right, and it went beyond what he could do for her body.

Faint intentions nudged the back of her mind. She should be doing something, give pleasure for pleasure. She slid her hands downward but they stopped over his chest, her fingers kneading his muscles while the pressure inside her built to the breaking point. A moan slipped from her lips as wave after wave of satisfaction washed over her body, cresting still when he cradled her against him.

Before she could catch her breath, he reached under her and shifted her slightly, then pushed inside her. The fullness of him nearly sent her over the edge again.

He rocked her, his hands splayed over her buttocks, massaging, squeezing, caressing. His lips found hers and they were gentle this time, almost reverent. He filled her to stretching, the slow rhythm he set making her want to jump out of her skin. He was holding back, teasing her. The sensation drove her mad.

She wanted fast and furious. She was ready. But he would not give it to her.

"We have all day," he said and nipped her bottom lip.

When she arched against him, he smiled.

Then she moved her hips in a deliberate circular motion and he grew serious.

"A battle of wills?" The strain in his voice betrayed what his restraint cost him. "I must warn you, the Bedu are legendary fighters. I come from a long line of warriors."

"So do I." She dipped her head to nip at his neck, tightening her inner muscles at the same time.

He groaned, but did not pick up the speed, shifted instead so he could reach even deeper. And there it was, that critical moment that comes in every battle when the outcome is decided.

She fought to win, with every weapon at her disposal.

She tightened her muscles around him, and again, hard quick squeezes even as she felt her own pleasure build to a peak. And he thrust inside her with force then, and pushed her over the edge.

Through the haze of complete satisfaction, she felt him shudder inside her body and empty himself into her. And she smiled.

Minutes passed before they were able to move. He took her with him to the carpets, cradled her in his arms. Their bodies depleted, their limbs intertwined, they rested.

She stared at the ceiling of the tent, trying to push her thoughts past the short-circuit in her mind. He had shocked her. Her own body had shocked her. She hadn't known it could be like this. Did other people?

"I feel like I discovered something," she said, turning to him. "Something enormous."

He came to his elbow to look at her, one eyebrow raised, a wide grin spreading on his handsome face.

Not too conceited, was he? Well, okay, with reason. "I mean like a lost city of legend in the desert. I feel like I should map the route or something and share with the masses. It seems unfair to keep it to ourselves."

"Sometimes it's good to be selfish," he said. "I'm keeping *you* for myself."

Her heart skipped a beat, but she ignored it smoothly and went on. "Not that I know how we got there, or if it ever could be done again."

"Oh, it can be done. I'm planning on sending many, many caravans there." He stood, surprising her.

Where did he get the energy? Her bones were still good and melted. As if knowing her inability to stand, he picked her up and carried her to the pool.

He walked in with her, lowering her into the cool water inch by inch. The water felt wonderful against her skin, almost as wonderful as Saeed's hands running down her body. He rearranged her slightly, pulled her against him, cupped her buttocks and lifted her. She wrapped her feet around his waist and felt the heat of his hardness nestled against her. "Another caravan so soon?" She toyed with his lips.

"Leaving immediately," he murmured.

HE COULD NOT GET ENOUGH of her. Saeed captured her mouth, rather than dwell on the unsettling thought. A part of him had already decided he would not let her go, while on another level he knew he must.

That he had brought her here, where he had never brought anyone, was insanity, perhaps even more—a betrayal of his tribe. But he trusted her, trusted her with his life.

When had that happened?

He kissed her lips, then tasted her fully, kept his gaze on her face, wanting to see her eyes darken when he slid into her tight, wet welcome.

She was like the water that surrounded them—a gift from above, necessary for survival.

He didn't like his need for her, the weakness of it.

She wasn't the right woman for him. She was a foreigner. An American. They had different backgrounds. She could never fully understand his family, his people. And he wasn't sure his people could ever fully accept her. Could Salah?

He was some kind of an assignment for her, nothing more. It cost him to remember that, but he could not afford to forget it, not even when every cell of his body was screaming for him to make her his. Forever.

He rubbed his hardness in a circular motion around her opening, watched her struggle for control then give up. And when he couldn't bear it any longer, he pushed into her quick and hard. He pushed deep, over and over, taking everything, wanting desperately to satisfy his hunger. When she moaned into his mouth, he drank the sound, and thought he could feel their souls merge until they were one.

He took her like a man possessed, wanting more than her body, wanting it all, wanting her to understand.

Then he felt her muscles tighten around him, squeezing him with sharp convulsions, and he pushed into her one last time, deep to her womb, and melted into her heat.

His knees were shaking as they clung to each other in the water.

When he felt steady once again, he washed her then carried her back to the tent. He wrapped her in silk and fed her meat and flat bread and dates. He watched her while she slept in his arms.

DARA AWOKE ALONE, but could hear him moving around in the back of the cave. She felt depleted physically and emotionally. And it wasn't just from the great sex—okay, once-in-a-lifetime-phenomenal sex—it was more. More had happened between them than the sharing of their bodies.

The question was—what was she going to do about it?

Nothing. Absolutely nothing.

Even if he wanted to go somewhere with this madness, she couldn't. She wasn't the settling-down type. She had lived in more places than she cared to count.

A long succession of military housing flashed through her mind.

She wasn't fit for long-term relationships. She had inherited that from her mother. It just wasn't in her. And that suited her fine—one of the things that made her a good candidate for the SDDU.

She had to extricate herself from this carefully with finesse, but with finality. She had to make sure Saeed knew that what had happened between them could never happen again.

The thought hurt, but she was tough. She was a soldier. She could handle it.

She glanced at her clothes, which were drying on the rocks by the pool, then wrapped a length of silk around her body.

"Is it time to go?" She walked to him, careful this time where she stepped.

"Almost." He riffled through the contents of a crate, closed it, started on another. He stopped when she reached him, drew her in and kissed her long and well.

She blinked her eyes and tried to clear her brain when he finally let her go. So much for keeping him at arm's length. But this was it, the last kiss, no more.

"What are you looking for?" she asked, all business, pleased with how together she sounded.

"Something light but valuable that we can take

back. What money Nasir keeps on hand for our *fakhadh* won't get us far without being able to access the rest in the banks."

"Don't you have foreign accounts?"

"Of course. But I don't have time to go to Europe to make withdrawals." He lifted out a sack and opened it.

She gasped at the sight of thumb-size gold nuggets.

"Too heavy," he said.

The next crate held ivory, the one after that jewels.

"How exactly did your grandfather come by this?"

"Most of it was passed down to him by our ancestors, although as I understand he did add to it before raiding became illegal." He pulled out a heavy bracelet, a flowering vine twisting like a spring, and pulled it on her right arm. The petals were made of sapphires, coming from a ruby center.

It distracted her for a moment.

"Your ancestors were bandits?" she asked when she recovered.

"Going on *razzia* was perfectly acceptable at the time. All Bedu did it. It so happens a couple of major caravan routes crossed through my ancestor's territory." He was more matter-of-fact than defensive, as he pulled out a ring, diamonds set in a circle of gold, and put it on her finger.

She had never been into jewelry, but somehow in

this place, with this man, it fitted. None of this was real anyway. They were in a dream—a fairy tale.

He searched some more and came up with a necklace that matched her bracelet, looped it over her neck, let the back of his hands caress her breasts when he laid the large pendant between them.

Her nipples just about poked through the material.

"The man had an eye for jewelry. His wives must have loved all this," she said to cover her embarrassment.

"One wife only, and my grandmother wasn't into baubles. She was a very sensible Englishwoman." He grinned at her.

She stared at him. "Your grandmother was English?"

He gave her a haven't-I-just-said-that look.

"Well, that explains the eyes."

He nodded. "I got her baby blues."

Baby blues weren't exactly the right description. His eyes were masculine and exotic, mesmerizing. She felt herself lean toward him, drawn by his gaze, but pulled herself back. "Your grandfather went to college in England, too?"

"Never set foot out of the country."

And then it occurred to her. But no, it couldn't be. The idea was too fantastic. "Are you saying he *stole* her?"

His handsome features stretched into a look of

shock. "That would have violated the *sharaf,* the Bedu code of honor. And above all, my grandfather was an honorable man."

She drew up an eyebrow.

"For your information, the Bedu are a lot more civilized than given credit for in the West. We do not steal women." He lowered his voice and added with a conspiratory wink, "We do not have to."

"Oh, please."

"Sanctity of women is an important part of our code of honor. Even in the old days of raiding, women and children were never harmed and enough camels and provisions were left with them to reach safety."

"So your grandmother came to your grandfather's tent, how?"

"She was the only woman in the caravan, traveling with her uncle who was trying to establish trade relations along the main caravan route that used to pass by not far from here. My grandfather was conducting a perfectly civilized, and at that time legal, raid to make up for animals lost in the severe droughts in the previous couple of years. The traveling English had a hard time parting with their possessions and put up an unnecessary fight. My grandmother was the sole survivor."

She shook her head. "And seeing how a Western woman could not get out of the desert on her own, out of the goodness of his heart, your grandfather took her into his protection."

"Exactly," Saeed said with a smile. "He was a very generous man."

"And I suppose he tried at once to return her to her country?"

He shrugged. "Well, not at once. Those were hard times, you understand, with the drought and all. They had to cover enormous distances just to find enough grazing to keep the herds alive. He didn't have time for travel right away."

"And by the time he could have taken her, his devilish charm had won her over?"

"Well, that. All the men in my family have that. If it weakens women, we are hardly responsible for it, are we?"

"Oh, for heaven's sake." She rolled her eyes, turning to walk away, but a small leather sack he pulled from the pile of jewels drew her attention.

It was a work of art, the leather barely visible under the intricate flower pattern made of turquoise beads of every size.

He untied the black silk string as she watched, and dumped the contents on his palm, lifted a long necklace, heavy almost to the point of a chain, with a more delicate string of gold hanging from it. A single thumb-size oval ring of gold hung on the end.

He went still, blinked, then looked at her with so much heat it took her breath away.

"Now, this is what I would really like to see you wear," he said, a dangerous light sparkling in his eyes. He held it out for her, and she took it, looping it around her neck.

"No. Not like that." He shook his head.

He snatched the silk from her body, the cool air of the cave a shock on her heated skin. She grabbed for the material but he held it out of her reach, so she dropped her arms and stood before him naked, letting him slip the chain over her shoulders until it came to rest on her hips.

"A belt?"

He nodded. "I think you are going to like it."

He adjusted the gold string with its medal to hang a hand width below her navel, nestled on top of the V between her thighs. Her nipples tightened, and from the way his eyes narrowed, she knew he had noticed.

She felt a thrill of excitement shoot through her. To wear jewelry under her clothes such as this, knowing it was for his gaze alone… But she could not sink into that fantasy. One of them had to maintain reason.

She stepped back, her naked bottom coming into contact with the rough surface of a crate. "Look I don't think we should—"

With a single movement he stepped after her, reached for the medal, and parted her flesh with his long fingers to place the gold ring against her most sensitive spot. Before she could protest, he rubbed the medal in a circular motion a couple of times then left it there, allowing her body to close over it.

Kaboom. The shock of her system going from zero to a hundred in two seconds left her gasping for air. The sensation was such exquisite torture, she could find no coherent thought in her mind, every nerve ending in her body alive and screaming for release.

Resolutions be damned, she moved forward and pressed against him.

"Not yet," he read the onslaught of desire in her eyes. "We have work to do."

He took her hand and led her forth to another stack of crates.

Each step, each movement, rubbed the medal against her, sending jolts of pleasure through her body, arousing her to the point of mindlessness. She wanted him and she wanted him *now.* But he would not relent. He inventoried his ancestor's treasure as if he had no care in the world, making her walk from pile to pile, from one end of the cave to the other.

"Ottoman gold coins." He lifted another long necklace. "You don't see many of these anymore. It is customary for a Bedu woman's jewelry to be melted upon her death."

She nodded weakly, and he dropped the necklace back into the crate and moved on. Her knees were trembling slightly now. If he wasn't leading her by the hand, she doubted she could have followed.

He looked through another crate, tipped another jar—silver coins this time.

"I don't suppose my ancestors were worried about weight back in the old days. Plenty of camels. But I can't put sacks of this stuff on Hawk's back. He already has to carry the two of us."

He moved on. "Maybe we should have brought camels. Ever rode one before?"

A few seconds passed before she realized he had asked her a question. She nodded, having no idea what that question had been.

He walked to a stack of small bamboo crates, used his knife to pry one open. The lid was stuck, some of the bamboo breaking before he succeeded.

"Empty," he said. "I wonder what had been in it."

She wondered if she was going to lose her sanity. Her body hummed with arousal, every nerve ending begging to be touched.

He pried off the seals from a few more jars, then he was done with the last one.

"Now," he said, as he lifted her onto the top of a large crate and shed his clothing.

She opened her legs for him, wet and needy, and he took her in one smooth thrust, medal still in place.

Sweet heavens.

It frightened her how completely he possessed

her, how he could push her to mindlessness in seconds. Her muscles quivered as she floated in a sky of pleasure, soaring higher and higher until she reached the stars.

And he made her reach them again, and again, and again.

"I wish we could stay here forever," he said after their hearts slowed.

Oh, hell, it was pure insanity. They could not keep this up. *She* could not keep this up.

She pulled away, forcing her mind back to reality, to the task they faced. "Your people need you more than I."

His sensuous lips curved into a smile. "Progress then, finally. You admit you need me."

He scared her, and she wasn't easily scared. She had to go, leave him now before it was too late and she couldn't leave him at all.

She slid off the crate without denying his words, slipping off one piece of jewelry after another. "When do we leave?"

"Now. Hawk is saddled." He would not take the gold from her when she held it out to him. "They're yours to keep."

She hesitated for a moment before setting them on top of the crate. "I can't." She walked away from him, fast, while she could, to find her clothes.

She didn't belong here. God help her, she was no

longer sure where she belonged. She drew a deep breath. She couldn't doubt herself now. She belonged to the SDDU. She was a soldier, not some lost soul like her mother.

"Can I help you to carry anything up?" she asked him when she was dressed.

He was closing the crates. He shook his head, went on to the tent, put a hand to one of the poles, then after a moment stepped away, leaving it standing.

"You first." He pointed to the opening in the wall, his mood strangely pensive.

She crawled through the narrow shafts, out into the twilight, and waited for Saeed, knowing he was probably sealing the passageways. When he finally pushed through the hole, he took care to conceal it with rocks. The rock slab they'd removed with Hawk's help was too heavy to move, and this time the horse couldn't help. They needed pushing not pulling.

He held his hand out for her once he was up in the saddle, and she took it and mounted behind him. She slipped her arms around his waist and held on as they rode.

The desert was as endless around them as the night sky above. Endless possibilities, endless dangers, endless opportunities for her to lose her way. Had she lost it already?

Out in the open with the magic of the cave left behind, it was easier to see how much they didn't belong together. The time they spent in the cave seemed like a dream, another world that did not fit with this one, with the here and now where they were riding to battle, where she was a U.S. soldier and his bodyguard.

She had broken the rules, both personal and professional. She had broken them big time.

It could cost her military career, the only thing she ever knew. She panicked at the thought. She didn't know how to be anything else but a soldier. It was an identity she had bought with blood, because more than anything in life she wanted someplace to belong without questions, unlike her mother, a lost leaf blowing in the wind, getting worn down and broken up.

The one thing she had consistently striven for since childhood was to avoid that weakness. To be strong like her father, to know with a certainty when her name was called who she was. Dara Alexander, United States Air Force. And now, the SDDU. She had reached as high as she could, had succeeded in her own world. Her father would have been proud of it had he lived to see.

But now, for the first time ever, she had broken the rules of the world she had sacrificed so much to belong to. And in truth, it could cost her more than her career. What she had done could cost her heart.

Within the next days or weeks, the fate of Beharrain would be decided. And then she would be recalled.

For a while, back at the cave, she had so lost herself in Saeed, in their bodies' response to each other, that she forgot everything else. Reality kept shifting like the sand. But she had to keep the upper hand or she would get sucked under and risk losing herself completely.

Chapter Eight

Nasir waited politely for Dara to withdraw from the tent.

"She stays." Saeed spoke in English to make sure she would understand, too.

The look of surprise on his brother's face turned into a look of shock. "Do you trust her?"

He nodded, just barely used to the idea. A week ago he would have never considered involving a foreigner in his affairs. "She is part of this now."

He gave Nasir time to accept Dara's new position. And Nasir did, nodding after a few moments of silence, trusting Saeed's judgment, giving unconditional support as he always had. They had disagreed from time to time, but Saeed had never had to wonder about Nasir's loyalty. His sibling had always been on his side. They would have given their lives for each other.

"Things have gotten worse since you left," Nasir

said after a while. "Word has gotten around that you were arrested. Some people thought you were killed, others thought you were still at the palace. A small group attacked the palace gates."

The muscles tightened in Saeed's jaw. He did not have to ask what had happened. Damn Majid. His royal cousin was a firm believer of ruling with an iron fist, paranoid of the chaos of civil war returning if he but showed the slightest leniency.

"They were massacred by the guards," Nasir said, confirming his fears. "People are rising up all over the country. Majid announced a state of emergency. His soldiers have surrounded every major school in the cities. He claims he wants to protect the students."

Anger rose in Saeed's chest. Anger and outrage. "He is holding the children hostage."

Although Beharrain was one of the more progressive Arab countries where girls were allowed an education, he knew which schools Nasir was talking about—the ones where the more well-to-do sent their sons, their heirs. The fathers would think twice about supporting the people who even now gathered in the streets, the lower classes who had nothing to lose.

A lot of the old nobility thought fondly of the time when Saeed's father had ruled, the peace and stability, the economic growth of the time. It stood in sharp contrast to the culture of corruption and fear they were living in now, when nobody could be certain when a knock on the door would bring a royal arrest warrant. A lot of people considered Ahmad's line the true line of succession. Faced with a choice between bringing back that legacy or living on with the current ruler, they would have supported Saeed.

Majid knew that. Hence the "securing" of the schools.

Saeed held out the small sack of loose diamonds and precious stones he had brought back from the cave. "You know where to go?"

Nasir caught the bag and nodded.

"Take enough men with you," Saeed said.

A couple of years ago, he would have known which families among the many tribes were rumored to have supplemented their herding income with gun sales. Now he spent too much time in the city to keep up with what went on outside his own tribe. As head of the confederation of tribes, the individual sheiks kept him up to date on the official events, but he had lost the intimate knowledge of his Bedu that came from desert living. And he missed it.

"The tribes are on the move?" he asked.

"Those who are with us will meet us in Tihrin." Nasir turned to leave.

"Go with Allah," Saeed called after him, hating to send him into danger.

"How big is the tribe?" Dara looked up from the map of Tihrin she'd been studying. She had stayed out of the conversation, he supposed, so she would not make Nasir uncomfortable. He appreciated her tact, that she wanted to make things smoother for him instead of expecting the kind of treatment someone else in her place might have thought herself entitled to.

"About two thousand men able to fight, fifteen to twenty thousand warriors in the whole confederation."

"And Majid's army?"

"Over a million."

She stilled. "Will they follow him?"

A good question. He thought for a moment. "The royal guard will fight to the death. The rest, I don't know." It was a drafted army, not of volunteers, many of the soldiers had family members who'd been killed when Majid had taken the throne, some with relatives still in prison.

"I need to make some calls," she said, the set of her mouth determined.

"I will not have Beharrainian blood shed on Beharrainian soil by foreigners." The words came out more heated than he had meant them to, but she needed to understand.

She hesitated. "There are other kinds of help. What do you plan to do?"

"Take the king as fast as we can. We cannot let the fight drag out. We cannot allow another civil war. If he is captured, the army might switch sides. He is not a popular ruler." He closed his eyes. "I do not want any of my people to die. Yet I must bring fight to Tihrin."

She stepped closer, but did not touch him. Nor had she allowed him to touch her since they had returned from the cave.

"That's why you'll make a good ruler," she said. "Because you care about the people. You don't seek the position for its inherent power, but you will take it because you want them safe."

He wondered if anyone else, even his brother, understood him as well as she did. He remained silent, hating the bloodshed he knew was to come.

"You don't have to do this alone," she said.

"There are things in this life a man must do alone."

"Coming into this world and going out of it. Everything in between gets better with teamwork." She gave him a thin smile. "My father used to say that."

"Sounds like a wise man."

She inclined her head. "Most of the time he was."

He wondered what his own father would do if he were still alive. Ahmad had been a shrewd ruler and flexible. He had laid the foundation of the Beharrainian economy by learning from the West. He was a master of compromise. He would have done absolutely anything to help his people.

"Call whomever you need." Saeed pointed to the cell phone on the carpet. "I want no bombs, no troops that shoot at everything that moves. But if they can help me to avoid as much killing as possible, I would welcome that assistance."

DARA LISTENED to the muffled voices that filtered through the divider, but didn't understand a single word. Everyone had gone to bed early—they had hoped Nasir would be back before midnight and they could leave for the city under the cover of the night. But it seemed nobody could sleep. Everything was ready. The men waiting.

She had spent the day going over the map of the city with Saeed, as well as the drawings he had made of the palace. They had assessed the building's strengths and weaknesses, and based on Dara's suggestions, had picked the points of attack.

The men had prepared for the coming fight, making sure all the vehicles were in good working order, pooling all the guns and ammo they had among them, and keeping up with the daily activities, too, taking out and bringing in the herds, so as not to give suspicion to Majid's small air force that was flying above, watching the desert.

Dara rested on the women's side of the tent and Saeed with her. She would not budge from that. Either he'd agreed or she would have come over to the other side with him and share that section with the dozen or so men to whom he was playing host. Six clans of his tribe had come to join him at Shelfa so they could drive to Tihrin together.

The women's side of the tent was quiet with just the two of them. Shadia, the servant woman, had gone to Saudi with Saeed's sisters and son. Dara hoped they had gotten there safely and were settled in by now.

"Where was your family that first night I was here? The tent was empty." She watched Saeed's handsome face in the light of the single lamp he'd lit.

"In Nasir's tent. I did not think they were safe with me."

"Because of the assassins?" She rose to her elbow. "But you left me to be attacked?"

"At the time I thought *you* might have been an assassin."

"Oh." He hadn't trusted his family with her. Couldn't blame him for that.

"I still should not have left you unprotected. If I hadn't come back in time—"

"I'm my own protection. I'm a soldier."

He fell silent for a while.

"Are you worried about the army?" According to the Colonel, satellite photos had revealed that Majid was sending troops into the desert.

"I worry about everything. There are no sides. Every man who dies tomorrow is my brother, whether he fights with me or against me."

What could she say to that?

"I wish you would stay with the women and children." He returned to the topic they had discussed several times that day.

"My orders are clear. I must stay with you. It might all be over tomorrow." The usual prebattle adrenaline coursed through her veins, but there was something else, too, this time, a strange reluctance that had never been there before.

Sure, she wanted to have the fight over with, but this time, she didn't look forward to being pulled out and returned home. And she worried about Saeed. He would be Majid's primary target. Everyone would be aiming at him.

"You should stay away from Tihrin and let the U.S. help you with Majid. They can drop in a small elite force that would hardly be noticed. The world would be none the wiser."

His expression hardened. "And play the coward? If I cannot gain leadership on my own, if enough of my people do not support me to win, I should not be king." He glanced away from her for a moment, then back, his gaze heated. "The country will be won by the will of my people and on the strength of my people. My honor does not allow any other way."

"Even if it means the fight might be more drawn out and more people die?"

He stayed silent for a moment. She could see him struggle with the answer.

"Freedom must be paid for—sometimes in blood—but nobody can pay the price for us. The people must know that they are strong enough to control their own destinies. Some things cannot be given on a platter as a gift. They must be earned."

She nodded reluctantly. There was logic in what he said, but still it seemed a lot like foolish pride to her. "The U.S. is a friend of Beharrain. Friends help friends in trouble. No loss of honor in that."

He shook his head. "The Cold War has been over for more than a decade. Russia is a friend to the U.S., right?"

"Sure."

"And after your dark days of terror when your country was in great pain and upheaval, would you have wanted friendly Russian forces to be deployed in your cities to help keep your country safe? How would American citizens have reacted to seeing armed Russian soldiers on their streets?"

She stared at him for a moment, the picture he painted unimaginable to her. "That's completely different."

"Is it?"

They both fell silent for a while.

"What would any foreign country want for their help?" he said then. "Because know this, nothing is free in this world, especially not when given to a country rich in oil. Would our rescuers want more influence in regulating the industry my nation depends on? Would they want to dictate policies and politics? If I was put onto the throne by others and not by my own people, to whom would I owe allegiance?"

"I worry about you," she blurted the truth at last.

And at that, his face relaxed and his lips stretched into a smile. "I worry about you, too. I wish also that you would stay behind."

"Not a chance."

He grew serious. "I know. I know this is what you do. I know you are capable of doing it. I accept it and won't hold you back. But don't expect me to ever be glad for it. The thought of any harm coming to you is like a knife slicing through my heart." He fell silent, then after a while, a playful glint came to his eyes. "If you came closer I could try to change your mind."

"Not a chance," she repeated, his words rattling her more than she cared to admit. She wanted to slip into his arms—anything could happen to either of them tomorrow. But she had to distance herself from him; she could not give in to whatever madness brewed between them. She wanted to take her heart with her in one piece when she left.

If it wasn't too late already.

"Scared of me, then? I promise I will not wear you out to the point where you'd be useless in fight. I don't like the idea of you going into battle, but I won't undermine you."

Somebody laughed in the other room, voices rose. Dara gave Saeed a pointed look. They weren't even alone, for heaven's sake.

He came to his feet with easy grace, held his hands out for her. "Let's go for a ride."

They should get some rest; the logical part of her brain knew that. But she could not for the life of her relax. She sat up, tucked her pistol into her waistband, and took his hand.

They walked barefoot through the dark camp, everyone but the guards asleep. The tents with their woven panels looked majestic in the moonlight—an ancient tradition, a way of life that could all too soon disappear. The poignant beauty of the Bedu and their way of life grabbed onto her heart.

"You probably think it's primitive," he said when he caught her looking.

"It reminds me of the summers of my childhood," she said, surprising herself. And all of a sudden she remembered the freedom of those summers, the wonder, the unbridled joy. She had forgotten that.

"You went camping a lot?"

"My grandfather was a Lenape, Native American. I used to spend the summers with him on the reservation." She couldn't remember the last time she'd shared that with anyone.

But she remembered the time well, starting when she was six, for about five years her mother had gone through a "returning to your roots" phase. Mom had gone back and forth between embracing and denying her heritage over the years, blaming every bit of bad luck on it, every job she lost, every time someone slighted her in any way, and for the fact that she could never muster up enough dedication to achieve anything in life.

He stared at her for a moment. "I think I would like to see that. How your people handle living the old and the new at the same time."

"Not well." She thought of the trailer park and the poverty. Her grandfather still had pride in who he was, but her mother had only complaints and disillusion.

"It is not easy." Saeed looked up at the sound of a plane going above. "I fear every day that too much is lost. And yet we must move forward or be forever left behind and overrun by an impatient history. There is no time to grow at our own pace. We must race to catch up with the rest of the world, and to gain speed we must toss many things overboard, things that are important to us," he spoke with a passion that reminded her of her grandfather when he spoke of his heritage.

"The only alternative is to be left behind and be exploited by the winners," Saeed said. "We must choose between our past and our future. It is not a choice anyone should have to make."

His words bounced around in her head, helping her understand him better and, more surprisingly, helping her understand herself. She glanced at the water truck and the sleeping camels next to it— generations colliding and the future of a nation at stake. It seemed too much of a burden for one man to bear.

"You can never lose this." She motioned with her hands to indicate their surroundings. "It's as much a part of you as your bones."

He did not respond at once, and when he did, his voice was low, inquisitive. "Have you not lost the Lenape?"

She blinked, surprised by the question, startled that he could see inside her so well. Had she? Heaven knows she had tried hard enough. The faces of her great-grandfather and grandfather rose in her mind, both of them dead now. She blinked a tear from her eye. She refused to cry. She was a soldier.

"For a time perhaps," she said. "You can't really lose yourself forever, can you?" She turned to him. "I mean, wherever you go, there you are." And for the first time she understood. And she felt comfortable with it.

They reached the horses and between the two of them they saddled Hawk swiftly. She rode in front of him, didn't protest when he enfolded her in his arms, leaning back into his strength while he spoke to one of the sentries before they rode into the desert.

"Is this safe?" she asked once the camp was out of sight.

"Majid's men are back at the city. He knows we're coming. It's too late for a covert assassination now. People would know what happened. They would rise up even without me." He nuzzled her neck.

"The king didn't send as many troops after you as I would have thought." She made a last ditch attempt at keeping her mind on something professional, on something a less distracted bodyguard should be thinking about.

"There is unrest everywhere. He couldn't afford to pull out of the villages. And a large contingent is stationed at the southern border. There's always trouble there."

She knew about the southern border. The Colonel had mentioned it, among other things. She expected to talk to the man again in the morning to get the latest satellite intelligence.

"Turn to face me." He was already lifting her as he spoke the words.

She swung her legs until she was sitting in the saddle face to face with him, her legs, having no other place to go, resting on his thighs. Now what? Not that she didn't like to be able to look into his eyes while they talked, but the position was hardly comfortable.

He let go of the reins to pull her close, touched his forehead against hers. "I've never known another woman like you."

She kissed him, afraid he might say more.

His lips parted over hers as he took charge, mastering her mouth as their bodies communicated what neither dared to put into words. He was gentle yet possessive at the same time, and thorough. Lord, he was nothing if not that.

He kissed her senseless, his hands roaming over her body, pulling her legs up until they were wrapped around his waist. She felt his desire and her body responded swiftly, heat pooling in her center that was pressed against his hardness.

And still he found ways to whip her arousal to new heights until she was ready to drag him to the sand, ready to beg for or take by force her release.

"Let me show you an old Bedu trick," he said against her lips and reached between them to unzip her pants.

"No," she said.

His hands stilled, his gaze full of emotions, confusion being prominent. "I don't know what's happening between us."

That wasn't what she needed to hear. She was conflicted on the issue already. His doubts weren't helping any. "We should not have gotten involved. I— It was my fault."

"This is not a mistake," he said with force.

"No," she sighed. However much it would hurt later, she would never regret it.

Why couldn't she have this with some nice American man? Preferably someone in the SDDU who understood her work and was on the same crazy schedule. Why did she have to fall for the one man with whom any relationship was completely impossible?

The last few days with him were like stepping on a live mine. She was still reeling from the explosion of sensations and feelings.

She wouldn't think about the feelings. Maybe she could distract herself with the sensations. Too soon the touch of his hands on her skin would be nothing but a memory anyway.

She wanted that closeness, their two bodies to be part of each other's one last time.

"About that Bedu trick—" She brushed her lips across his.

"Mmm?"

"Maybe you should show me. I mean, for the sake of cultural exchange."

He cut off with a kiss whatever else she might have babbled. He moved her legs until he could slip off everything—an involved process, but he managed without making her feel awkward—careful to tuck her clothes behind the saddle. Then came his garments, although by that time she barely noticed what he was doing with his hands since his lips were closed around her nipple.

He cupped her buttocks and he let go of the nipple to take her lips as he pulled her up and forward onto his lap, onto him.

She moaned as he stretched her, filled her with instant pleasure. He had spoiled her for life, she thought. Nobody would do after him. She was going to die an old maid—a very, very horny old maid.

"You like this?" he asked with a conceited grin.

"You're a regular circus act." She tightened her legs around his waist and drew him in deeper, flashing a smirk of her own at the stunned look that appeared on his face.

The saddle moved back and forth with the gait of the horse, and they with it. All other movement on their part was unnecessary, nothing to do but enjoy the steady rhythm and let their hands discover each other's bodies.

The wild pleasure his body gave her took her by surprise each time. So did his gentleness. It had never been this way for her with anyone.

When they were like this, the world disappeared around them. She didn't want it to return. He was an addiction, a compulsion. Somewhere along the way her body had become convinced that he was necessary for her survival, and overrode her mind.

She refused to worry about tomorrow, the next hour, the next minute even. She just wanted to enjoy the here and now. She wanted to savor every moment of their time together, preserve it forever in her memory and take it with her when she left.

She would not think that this might be the last night they spent together. She would not think beyond the pleasure of the very moment they were sharing.

He kissed her lips, long and tender as the horse plodded on, taking them on to new heights of ecstasy.

"I like the Bedu ways," she gasped out the words as tension tightened her body. She felt the first spasm of her muscles then felt him surge inside her as they rode into mindless bliss together.

NASIR DIDN'T COME BACK until dawn, forcing them to wait another day so they could have the cover of darkness as they approached the city. The old hand-me-down B-52s Majid's air force used weren't equipped with night vision. The Bedouin army meant to take advantage of that weakness, but the waiting was hard. Tension and impatience vibrated in the camp. The men were ready to fight.

Dara looked over the small hill of weapons piled in the tent that had had to be enlarged to hold them all and shield them from the prying eyes above. Crates of semiautomatics, hand grenades, grenade launchers, blocks of TNT. Everything brand new, standard military issue. The little hairs on the back of her neck prickled. She glanced at Saeed, who was talking to the elders of the clans.

She wanted to be by his side, but understood that it would hold him back. He needed to be with his men, strengthening alliances and reinforcing connections. The presence of a foreigner, especially a woman, would be in the way.

For a moment, she wondered if she would ever be fully accepted in his world, then it occurred to her how little it mattered. She would not be in his world much longer.

She ambled toward him and caught his gaze. He came over a few minutes later.

"Miss me?" He flashed her a cocky grin. "I promise to give you lots and lots of undivided time once we take the palace."

She snorted to cover up the fact that her blood raced at the thought of them spending some private time together in the near future. "You are the father of your people. Get your mind out of the gutter and try to act with some decorum."

He raised an ebony eyebrow. "You want to talk about the attack?"

She shook her head. "Where did Nasir buy these weapons?"

Saeed looked at her for a moment as if he didn't fully comprehend the question. "He has connections."

"Smugglers?"

He drew back at the disapproval in her voice. "It's hard to make a living from the herds anymore. Not all Bedu have oil."

"You sent your brother to the same gun smugglers who supply the terrorists?" A sense of betrayal choked her. Damn it. He was supposed to be one of the good guys.

"The world is spotted," he said, not looking the least bothered.

"Excuse me?"

"It's an old Bedu saying. It means the world is full of good and bad. Every action has many consequences. Without the weapons, I cannot defeat Majid, but by obtaining weapons I gave money to the illegal gun trade." He fell silent for a moment. "You should understand hard choices."

"Well, I don't understand how you could make this one."

He took a deep breath. "While hunting terrorists in Afghanistan, the allied forces made over five thousand accidental kills. That's the number of innocent people who were taken out by accident, a number the Pentagon publicly admitted. But it doesn't mean that going after the terrorists was wrong. It was right and necessary, and yet, in another aspect, a terrible price had to be paid."

Heat crept into her face and voice. "Damn it, don't

you tell me about that. I was there. I flew twenty-two missions." She swallowed. "I probably killed some of those innocent people."

"You did what you had to do and in the end you probably saved the lives of ten times as many," he said quietly.

She looked at him for a while, then back at the trucks. "You are breaking the law."

"I am about to lead a rebellion. In case you haven't noticed, this whole enterprise is illegal."

"The men your brother is doing business with are probably the same ones who shot down my plane and killed my team." She heard her voice rise as Harrison's and Scallio's faces flashed into her mind, Miller's.

"Your plane had no business being in Beharrainian airspace," he said, but there was no heat in his words.

"So you're glad it was shot down?" Anger whipped through her.

"I'm glad I found you," he said quietly.

The look in his eyes took the wind out of her sails for a second.

"When you're king—"

"When I'm king my first priority will be to make the desert safe again. I'm going to make sure that all the tribes can survive and make a living legally, so they don't have to turn to smuggling."

She gave him a skeptical look.

"'The country we build, we build it for our sons.' My father used to say that. I *will* uphold the law."

And it filled her with relief to know he meant it.

"I cannot win against Majid with daggers and the few old rifles that have been handed down from father to son in the tribe."

He couldn't. She knew that. But damn it, he could have asked her for help. She could have had the Colonel arrange for a weapons drop. "I'm going to need to talk to Nasir and get as much information as possible."

"He is my brother." Saeed's voice carried a fair dose of warning.

She held his gaze.

"We will go together," he said.

"Did you get the TNT from the same people?" Dara watched as Nasir's face hardened. He disliked being questioned by a woman, answered her only because Saeed was there.

"Of course. I didn't have time to wander all around the desert shopping. I was lucky to get any at all. They were taking a big shipment to the border for someone. It cost me plenty to have them give me even a little of it."

"Which border?" She figured Yemen.

"Saudi," he said.

Saeed sat up straighter. Dara understood his sudden focus. His sisters and son were in Saudi.

"If there was a large-scale terrorist attack, what would be the obvious choices? The U.S. embassy, company compounds with Western interest, U.S. Air Force bases."

"Call Gedad and warn him, just in case," Saeed said to Nasir as he stood. "I'm sending men for Salah, Fatima and Lamis."

Dara held her hand out for his cell phone. "I'm calling this in."

Saeed dropped the phone into her palm. "Nasir will tell them everything he knows."

And from the look he pinned his brother with, she was pretty sure Nasir would.

Chapter Nine

Majid looked up as the door opened. "Any news, Jumaa?"

The prime minister bowed. "The tribes are moving around, but not uniting."

"Not as stupid then as I had thought," Majid said with some relief. He had the air force out with orders to bomb anything that looked suspicious, take out any gathering force. A good chunk of his army, as many men as he could spare, was set up a few miles from Tihrin to catch any small groups that might escape the air force's attention and think to march on the city. "And my cousin?"

"Still missing. Perhaps we should let him be. He is too popular right now. Once things settle down, he could meet with an accident." Jumaa worried his beard with his stubby fingers.

He was nervous. Majid watched him as a hawk watched its prey. Jumaa was weakening. He did not understand how important it was to have Saeed out of the picture. He understood little, but knew too much—a liability.

Majid reached for the carafe and poured coffee in two china cups, sprinkled something extra on Jumaa's.

They drank, and he watched the man go pale as the first muscle spasm squeezed his chest. Majid reached for the cup, not wanting the five-hundred-year-old Persian carpet beneath their feet soiled. "Are you all right?"

Jumaa took a handkerchief from his pocket, wiped off the beads of sweat from his forehead. "Please excuse me—"

"No need for an apology. Should I send for a physician?"

"No…yes." The man clutched his chest.

Majid picked up the phone and ordered the royal physician to be sent to his office at once, knowing that before the doctor even got the message, Jumaa would be dead.

He watched the man slide down in his chair, gasping for air as his eyes rolled back in his head. He waited until the last tremors left the prime minister's body, then left the room.

Something in watching others die made him feel more alive, a heady feeling that had him seek out the torture chambers from time to time. He smiled as he crossed the reception room, his body humming with energy.

He was in a good mood, pleased to see his youngest wife and latest son coming through one of the many doors.

"Come." He went to his favorite sitting room and when they followed, he motioned to the nanny to bring the child closer. Yes, he appraised the boy, he would be a strong son. He had many and needed many more. They were the only ones he could fully trust. He wished they would grow faster.

"Leave us." He turned from the nanny and focused on his wife.

She bowed, trembling slightly, the very picture of submission. He found it arousing.

"I thought I might leave the palace today to shop for our son," she said, her voice tentative, unsure. "If you would give permission and select the guards to come with us."

He barely heard the words as he ran his fingers over her perfect breasts, enlarged with milk. He turned her and pushed her against the desk, bent her face down, lifted her dress up, ripped her pants with impatience.

She parted her legs obediently and he shoved into her quick and hard, one hand on her hip, the other squeezing a firm nubile buttock.

Three thrusts and he erupted into her, the powerful burst making him dizzy for a moment, then he stepped away, pulled up his pants.

"You may go shopping tomorrow. I don't want you to lose my seed by walking all over the city. Go rest," he said.

The phone rang just as she was closing the door behind her. At first he ignored it, resenting the intrusion into his moment of bliss, but then he picked up the receiver. Too much was going on in the country, the stakes too high, and he was the only one who could make everything work out right.

He listened to the man on the other end and smiled, glad he decided to take the call. "His son? Are you sure?"

SAEED HELD DARA IN HIS ARMS in the back room of the tent. He could not sleep, but instead spent the hours thinking over their plans, looking for any possible flaw, any opportunities they might have overlooked. They were to leave camp between 1:00 and 2:00 a.m. and get to the city just before dawn.

He had called Gedad's house twice, but got the answering machine both times. They were probably in bed already. His sisters' cell phones were turned off for the night. He should have told them to leave the phones on at all times until this was over. It didn't matter now. His men should be there soon to take them to safety. He missed the boy. Worried about him, too, although he knew his son would be kept safe. Still, he hated the idea of them being apart; the frustration of it ate at him.

Dara stirred in his arms, drawing his attention to another concern. He hated the idea of her going into battle with him, but struggled to accept it. He must because this was who she was. She would come to Tihrin to protect him, and he would do everything in his power to protect her.

"Once we have Majid, the fight will be over fast," she said.

"You're awake."

"You're worrying." She burrowed her face into his neck.

"Just thinking over our plans."

Taking the fight to Tihrin, the king's stronghold, was risky business, but had many advantages. For one, the air force could not fight them. Majid would not order the bombing of the city. Not while he was still in it.

A plane went overhead. They were covering the desert all day, but so far they had not attacked. All military equipment was carefully hidden in tents, the encampment appearing like any other ordinary clan on the move with its grazing animals. Orders went out for lighting no fires during the night.

Saeed's cell phone rang, and when he took the call, a strange man's voice came through.

"It's for you." He handed Dara the phone, and waited while she listened to whoever was on the other end.

She sat up. "If there's any news of a five-year-old

boy, Salah ibn Saeed and his aunts Fatima and Lamis—"

His heart stopped as she spoke the names.

"Yes, thank you," she said and handed the phone back to him.

The line was dead. "What happened?" Fear squeezed his heart.

"The U.S. Air Force base over the border was attacked by terrorists about half an hour ago. There's some damage, much less than there would have been had we not warned them."

He was dialing Gedad's number as she talked. The phone beeped, went dead and then the dial tone came back on again. He got to his feet. "I'm going over there."

"The Colonel is going to order a priority search for your family. He will let us know as soon as there's any news."

He swallowed. He was too far, damn it.

"There's more," Dara said. "It seems there is a connection between Beharrain and the attack. It's been arranged from the very top."

That brought him up short. It couldn't be, could it? His cousin was not the most scrupulous man, but surely he was not a terrorist. What would he gain by such an act? Why try to disable an American Air Force base?

Unless he was planning on doing something he was worried the Americans would interfere with.

"Satellite pictures show the entire Beharrainian army has mobilized. Would he attack Saudi?"

Saeed shook his head. "It would make no sense. They're twenty times bigger than us and armed to the teeth."

"Yemen?"

He nodded, remembering Majid's resentment of the borders established by the international community that he claimed had dissected his heritage. Majid had always thought of the entire southern desert as his, legacy of the larger-than-life great-grandfather he idolized.

Majid was on the brink of thrusting the country into war. And they were in no shape for it, neither their people nor their army. Saeed had a clearer picture than his cousin, whose generals feared him enough to tell him only what he wanted to hear.

Tens, perhaps hundreds of thousands would be dead for nothing. He had to stop Majid, had to get to him before he ordered the troops on the southern border to attack. Once war broke out, nobody would be able to stop the killing.

But his son and sisters needed help, too. He reached for Dara's hand in the darkness. "Can I trust your people with my family?"

Her response was instant and sure. "As you trust me."

It wasn't easy for him. But he did trust Dara. And

his people needed him, all of his people. He wrapped his kaffiyeh around his head. "We leave for Tihrin right now," he said.

THE MOTLEY BEDOUIN ARMY crept across the desert without headlights. A wisp of a cloud that would evaporate soon enough once the sun came up covered the moon, giving them further advantage. Some of the vehicles had been hidden at a nearby oasis, a number of pickups pulled into tents during the day. Now that they didn't have to worry about raising suspicion and all came together, they made a respectable size convoy.

Dara peered into the darkness, hoping to glimpse the lights of the city. They skirted Majid's army without trouble, thanks to continuous intelligence received from the Colonel, who arranged for drones to keep an eye on troop movements.

According to the intelligence reports, the royal palace was fortified to keep out the angry mob that was gathering on the streets, but there was no major deployment in the city beyond that. Majid clearly expected to annihilate Saeed's tribal forces in the desert and for the rest of his people to accept the defeat and back down.

Saeed stared forward as he drove the truck, his face grim, but his resolve evident in his gaze. "You're adamant about fighting?"

"Damn right," she said. "Do you have a problem with that?"

"It drives me crazy."

"Get over it."

He looked at her, his expression pained. "I'm trying."

"I fight for a living. I'm a soldier."

He turned his attention to the sand before them. "If truly you were a soldier, you wouldn't have to remind yourself so often."

A quick protest died on her lips. She truly was a soldier, wasn't she? In her heart? Or was she following the path set before her by her father? Was she striving for his approval still?

"If I'm not a soldier, who the hell am I?" She was disturbed by the idea and angry at him for suggesting it.

"That's something only you can find out. Have you ever wanted to do anything else?"

"Never." Everyone she knew growing up had worked for the air force, except for her mother who'd been a housewife and miserable because of it. Dara had sworn she would never put herself into that situation.

So had she chosen the service because that was what she really wanted, or because she didn't know anything else?

"Hell of a time to make me doubt myself. In the middle of a freaking offensive!"

He took her hand, held it. "You should never doubt yourself. You're strong, intelligent, determined. You can succeed at anything you want. Maybe you should ask yourself why you became a soldier in the first place."

That was easy—to be like her father, to pattern herself irrevocably after him and to make sure she didn't end up with the identity crisis of her mother.

"You just don't want me to be a soldier because you don't think a woman should be," she said sullenly, not at all appreciating his insight.

He opened his mouth, but she cut him off. "If you say women should be cherished, I'm going to scream."

He threw her a reproaching look. "I was about to say that I don't want you to be a soldier because it scares the soul out of me. But if this is what makes you happy I'll learn to live with it."

She stared at him, digesting the words, which implied they would have a relationship beyond the next few days, a relationship during which he would have to learn to live with her occupation.

Oh yeah, that would go down well. If the Colonel found out she'd had an affair with the man she was supposed to protect, she would probably be court-martialed. Could she be court-martialed for sleeping around on the job? She needed to check into that.

"We're here," he said.

When she looked up, she could see the lights of a few dozen high-rises in the distance.

As agreed before they'd left camp, the trucks and pickups spread out, preparing to enter the city through as many points as possible. All the tribes had specific tasks. Some were to go to the schools Majid was keeping under lockdown, others secured the streets. The goal of Saeed's team was to surround the royal palace as quickly as they could.

But trouble started before they even reached the paved streets. Fire opened on them from several rooftops. Bullets tore up the road around them. Men fell.

Those still alive charged forward, rushing into the coverage of the houses. A couple of trucks stopped and men ran to take care of the rooftop shooters. People were coming out to the streets to see what was going on. Then Saeed was recognized and word spread.

He drove straight for the palace, and his people took key positions, waiting for his word to attack. Capturing Majid was the key to swift victory with as little bloodshed as possible.

The clouds had thickened and covered the moon, but the streetlights provided plenty of visibility as they got out of the truck.

Dara felt the first fat raindrop on her face, and glanced at Saeed who looked like he'd just received a sign from heaven. She didn't like the timing, but for his people's sake she hoped they would have a good rain this year, more than the previous winter when, according to Saeed, a three-hour rainstorm in one afternoon had been all the water they'd gotten.

The rain picked up and she looked at the upturned faces around her, watching the pleasure and optimism the people soaked up from the sky. Then Saeed moved forward, and a wave of desert warriors followed him as one.

They came under increasingly heavy fire as they moved toward the palace, but their number had grown. Some of the other tribes had arrived. Dara looked around at the sea of people, most of them on foot. They came from every section of the city, woken by gunfire.

"Ready?" she asked Saeed, and he nodded.

She checked the twenty pounds of TNT in the back of the SUV, fixed the gas pedal and aimed the car toward the barricades at the palace gate, tying the steering wheel in position. She reached through the window and put the shift in gear before jumping clear of the vehicle.

The people who knew of the plan were taking cover. It took but a few seconds for the rest to figure out what was going on and join them.

The explosion started every car alarm within a mile and blasted out half the palace windows. Dara shook broken pieces of glass from her hair as she charged ahead from behind the abandoned car they had used for cover. From the corner of her eye, she could see Saeed doing the same.

The fight was bitter, every step of progress bought with blood. Saeed had been right. The royal guard did not give up easily. But Saeed's men were just as loyal and determined. It took fifteen minutes of heavy gun-fight to take the gate, another half hour to reach the first corridor. The plan was to trap Majid in his private quarters.

She followed Saeed and took out two men who came at them guns blazing from a side passage. She moved on as fast as she could but not so fast as to be careless, mindful that they were on Majid's territory.

Saeed reached a door to the left, opened it and burst in as she covered him. Nobody in there. They kept going. The sounds of chaos reached them from the courtyard. She hoped the other teams who were sent to circle behind the king's private rooms and cut off his escape routes were making progress.

She heard a door slam open ahead of them, then royal guards flooded the hall. Saeed jumped into the cover of a doorway and pulled her with him, firing nonstop at the men. *Here we go.* She went down on one knee so they wouldn't be in each other's way.

They were outnumbered, but Saeed and she were better shots, thinning the group quickly. Then one of the guards threw a grenade. He had to have been holding onto it for a while because it blew the second it hit, not leaving her time to draw back.

She sank to the ground, blinded and half-deaf.

"Are you hurt?" She heard Saeed's words as if from under water.

She nodded, the small movement making her dizzy. She blinked her burning eyes a couple of times. Everything was bright white with a smattering of shadows. Her throat constricted.

"I can't see," she said panicked, and felt Saeed's hand on her arm, pulling her up.

He patted her down. "Your clothes are torn in a couple spots. You have some cuts and scratches but I don't see any serious injuries. Can you move everything?" His voice was tight.

"I think so." A miracle. She should have been dead. The hallway was quiet. "Did you get them?"

"Most of them. The rest retreated."

"We can't stay here."

"You can't go anywhere like this."

She reached out and grabbed onto his belt. "Keep going. I'll be better in a minute. Just blinded by the flash, that's all."

She gripped his leather belt with one hand, her rifle with the other, then heard gunfire. Saeed pushed her aside to respond, but she refused to let him take on the danger on his own. She might have been temporarily disabled, but she wasn't useless yet. Blindly, she angled the AK-47 around him and shot in the direction of the sound.

"You are an exceedingly stubborn woman," he said and pulled her on.

"You said that before."

"It bears repeating."

"Where are we?"

"In one of the reception rooms. We're close."

"And if he's not in his bedroom?"

"If he's in the palace, he is there, and I think he's in the palace. We haven't given him enough warning to get away and he is too conceited to consider we'd get this far. His bedroom is reinforced. No windows. The walls are made of Kevlar."

Like a panic room, she thought, and blinked her eyes a couple of times, impatient with them. Her vision was returning, but too slowly. She could see Saeed's form in front of her, the larger pieces of furniture like menacing shadows looming against the walls.

She heard footsteps behind them, turned, aimed her gun.

"Ours." Saeed pushed the barrel down.

They moved forward.

Her ears were still ringing but not too badly. She could once again hear the sound of gunfire that came from all over the palace.

By the time they reached the gold double doors,

she could see enough to let go of Saeed and tell apart friend from enemy.

A good thing, as royal guards rushed them from a side door. She went down onto her stomach behind a console and, using it for cover, took aim, squeezed the trigger and didn't let go.

One royal guard fell after the other, not having much to hide behind in the open doorway. But there were a lot of them, too many, a new one always ready to step into place.

Saeed was next to her, and in the cacophony she reserved a compartment of her brain to listen for nothing else but the sound of his gun, knowing that as long as he was shooting he was alive.

Men she knew from camp lay dead around them. She fired on, dreading the moment when she would have to reload, afraid they could press even that moment of an advantage. Most of the shooting came from the royal guards, the guns of Saeed's men falling silent one after the other.

They were used to hunting with old Winchesters, not this kind of desperate hell of a shootout with semiautomatics. She squeezed off her last shot, pulled back behind the console and switched magazines while Saeed covered her.

Then she was back, not aiming at any organ or anyone even in particular, her vision still blurry, but spraying the enemy with bullets.

And at last when the four in the doorway fell, no others came to take their place.

The men who rushed in a few minutes after that were Saeed's. They tried to bust the double doors, using the butts of their rifles then heavy pieces of furniture, but to no avail. The doors held, even after Dara shot up the locks.

"Probably barricaded from inside," she said, and Saeed nodded, then called out loudly in Arabic.

She only understood two words, *Majid* and *TNT,* but they were enough to know what he was saying. He was threatening the king with blowing him up if he did not come out.

An empty threat since what little explosives they'd had, they'd used up at the gate.

Silence followed his words, then a few words, spoken by a child.

Saeed went white. "He has my son."

The men with him looked as stricken as he did. He called out something in Arabic again.

"La," came the response.

This, she understood—*no.*

The man on the other side of the door spoke again. She turned to Saeed for translation.

"He says if we don't leave the palace at once, Salah will die. He will not negotiate."

Dara looked at the pain on his face, then stepped forward and raised her voice. "My name is Dara Alexander, I am here on behalf of the United States government. I want to discuss the terms of truce."

Silence followed her words, then after a while the same one-word answer Saeed had gotten earlier. *"La."*

"I will come in unarmed. I'm sure you're not afraid of a woman."

No response.

"You have nothing to lose by letting me in. You'll have one more hostage."

Saeed reached for her arm to pull her back.

God, he was never going to let her do this. He hated to rely on others. He wasn't going to put his son's life into the hands of a foreigner, a woman at that. "You must trust me. He will never let you in. I can do this," she said, desperate for him to understand.

"I know." His gaze bore into hers. After an eternity, he nodded. "You can do anything."

She smiled, knowing well what it cost him to let her handle this, appreciating the vote of confidence.

The door opened a crack, a rifle barrel pushed through. Dara walked up to the opening and was pulled inside roughly, the door closing behind her with a bang.

Along with King Majid and the boy, a dozen royal guards were in the room, as well as Saeed's sisters, huddled in the corner, scared out of their wits. Odd that Majid hadn't mentioned them. Or maybe not that odd. He probably thought little of their value for bargaining or otherwise, since they were women.

Dara watched the king while one of the guards searched her. Majid looked nothing like Saeed, despite their relation. He was shorter, with a wide face and a prominent mustache that hung over fleshy lips. He was not overweight, but clearly out of shape.

Her gaze slid back to the hostages and she smiled at Salah and Saeed's sisters, hoping to reassure them. She could see fairly well now, and was grateful for it. She looked around the room for any possible strategic advantage.

King Majid's bedroom was bizarre in its excess. Frescoes of nudes decorated the high ceilings, framed with gold molding. Priceless art covered the walls, life-size marble statues of naked Roman goddesses in every corner, despite the fact that religious law strictly forbade any depiction of the human body. The furniture looked like something antique dealers would call *Louis* with a number after it.

The room had two other exits and judging from the fact that Majid was still here, she guessed they were blocked by Saeed's men from the outside.

"Say what you came to say," the king ordered in his accented English.

"Release your hostages and you'll be guaranteed safe passage to the country of your choosing for exile, as long as they agree to take you."

She could make no such guarantee in Saeed's name nor in her own government's, but she didn't expect Majid to go for it anyway. She was just buying time until she figured out what to do.

"I can stay here until my army returns to the city and crushes the rebels."

"Your army defected," she said without blinking.

She could see a moment of hesitation in his small brown eyes.

"I will not be run off. I'll die as a hero and take Saeed's heir with me."

"What would that accomplish?" she asked, her voice calmer than she felt. "Sheik Saeed will have another heir and you will be dead."

Rage contorted the man's face. He was clearly not used to anyone resisting him, especially not a woman.

She inched toward the guard to her left, the one who kept his eye on Fatima instead of the proceedings. If she could grab his gun, it might give her some leverage. If she was able to get her hands on Majid, she was pretty sure her demands for the guards to surrender would be met.

But before she could go for it, another guard burst through the wall, panting and bloody, bowing then talking rapidly.

She stared at the man's point of entry. A hidden wall panel. Damn. Saeed didn't know about that.

"It seems my men secured a way out of here. I have loyal troops on the southern borders. I'll be back in the palace within a week and we'll see who will be dead then." Majid grabbed Salah by the arm and dragged him to the open panel, his guards pulling Fatima and Lamis to their feet to follow.

Damn. Dara glanced toward the golden double doors. One of the guards raised a rifle to her head. She couldn't risk calling out to warn Saeed. She couldn't afford to get shot. She needed to go with the hostages to save them.

She watched as the small party stepped through the open wall panel and followed obediently, thinking of the knife tucked in her boot and that the farther from the rebel forces the king got, the more he'd lower his guard.

They passed through a long corridor. When Salah tripped on the uneven ground, Majid yanked his arm and yelled at the child.

"Let me carry him," Dara said. "We'll go faster."

After a moment of hesitation Majid nodded. She picked up the boy, and he hid his face in the crook of her neck. He couldn't have weighed over forty pounds. She had carried rucksacks heavier than that for days at a time on exercise.

They reached a hidden doorway and descended three flights of stairs, then entered a dark cramped passageway, the walls built of stone—an escape tunnel probably built for just this purpose. She watched the way the men moved, seeking to judge their strength, whether any of them had sustained injuries.

There were only ten guards now, Majid had left two back in his bedroom, to hold Saeed off as long as possible, no doubt.

They walked on for a long time, crossed over to the sewer system at one point; Dara sniffed at the sharp smell of ammonia in the air. She was glad when the corridor finally angled upward. When they came to a doorway, one of the guards busted off the padlock from the door with the butt of his rifle. A steep staircase led upward, and they followed it to a stainless-steel-covered room.

Two large metal tables stood in the middle; small square doors in even rows lined the walls from floor to ceiling. A morgue? She didn't have time to look around. The guards rushed the hostages through the room and up another set of stairs. Bandages, all kinds of medical equipment. Looked like they were in the storage area of some kind of hospital.

Three of the men ran forward and disappeared from sight. When the rest of the group caught up, they were in the ambulance bay, a half-dozen bodies on the floor.

The king climbed in the back of an ambulance, and Fatima and Lamis were pushed after him, then Dara and Salah. That didn't leave much room for guards, but six managed to squeeze in. She figured two would sit up front, that made eight professional soldiers she had to take care of. She wasn't overly worried about Majid.

But she couldn't do anything yet, not when a flying bullet might hit one of the people she was here to protect. She had to wait, bide her time, be ready when the opportunity came.

Chapter Ten

Dara leaned back against the wall of the ambulance and inventoried the weapons around her. Each man had a semiautomatic, with extra magazines. Majid had a pistol tucked into his belt.

The siren came on, and Salah, who'd gone to sit between his aunts, covered his ears.

Dara smiled at him. "Everything is going to be okay."

She fell silent when the soldier next to her raised his rifle. Looked like they preferred if she didn't talk.

Too bad.

She made sure to keep the smile on her face for the boy's sake while her mind worked at full speed. The farther they got from the city and Saeed's forces, the less Majid would need the hostages. Once he felt safe, would he get rid of them?

"You should leave them behind." She nodded toward Saeed's sisters and son.

The king looked at her, angry and impatient. "You should shut up."

"Saeed will pursue his heir to the ends of the world. Any man would. If you let the boy go, finding you becomes much less important, giving you time to regroup."

The king said nothing, but he was listening.

"Salah is the great-great-grandson of Sheik Zayed, your own blood. If something happens to him, the people will not forgive it easily, even if it's not your fault. We could come under fire. Everyone will blame you if he dies."

Majid looked away from her.

"Let them go and keep me," she said.

He snorted with derision. "What good would you be? If I need to bargain, I'll need something of value. What will Saeed give me for the life of a foreigner, a woman?"

She weighed her words carefully. "Some men are attached to their mistresses."

Majid's gaze snapped back to her. He measured her up. "He *is* the type to get attached to a woman— a weakness that runs in his family. Took but one wife and didn't take another even after her death."

She watched him as he rubbed the heels of his hands over his knees, and could see the wheels turn in his head, as he considered how to exploit Saeed's weakness.

"If what you say is true…" He watched her closely.

"Why do you think he keeps me by his side at all times? He cannot bear to be separated from me even when he goes to battle. Saeed will give for me what you ask of him," she said with false confidence.

A muscle ticked in his cheek.

She stayed silent for a while, not wanting to push him into a rage where he might cross over into violence.

"They know you had a hand in the bombing at the air force base," she said when she thought he was calm enough again.

He went still, his face cold and frozen like the statues in his bedroom.

"The U.S. is looking for you, too. Everyone will be searching for a small group of soldiers with a couple of women and a small boy with them."

She left time for her words to sink in before she went on. "With a kaffiyeh on, nobody can tell me from another soldier. You'll get much farther with just me. And the Americans will negotiate for me should anything happen. They don't like to lose one of their own. Bringing home body bags makes for bad publicity. It's bad for politics." She watched him closely. "Let them go."

"Do not," he said in a voice of ice, "presume to tell me what to do."

MAJID WATCHED THE WOMAN, angered and at the same time aroused by her fire. Under different circumstances, he would have enjoyed bringing her to heel and bedding her. Mastering a willful woman took skill, like mastering a willful horse. Of course, with his horses he would have never used unnecessary force. His stable of purebred Arabians was too valuable.

He appraised Dara. This one would require force. He would enjoy it. Maybe they would have some time for that kind of fun when he was out of danger, surrounded by his army once again.

He trusted his southern troops; they didn't have as many Bedu among them as among the troops that had defected according to the woman. He believed her on that. But the troops stationed on the southern border… Everything hinged on them.

His confidence wavered.

If they thought Saeed was winning, would they have thrown their support behind him already? Could he risk it?

Fear gripped him for a moment, the fear of having nowhere to go. Then he pushed it back. There was one place, one people who stood to lose if Saeed took the throne. Majid breathed easier, with renewed confidence. He would hide among them until he figured out who was still loyal to him.

HE SHOULDN'T HAVE LET Dara go in there. All they'd accomplished was giving Majid another hostage. She had asked him to trust her, and he did—she was smart and strong, amazing—but by Allah, it had cost him to let her go to Majid.

Saeed tried to listen for voices but the doors were soundproof, as were all doors in the king's private quarters. They would have to be yelling to be heard.

"Either you open that door or I am breaking it," he called out, and he meant it.

No response.

His heartbeat quickened. "I'm offering to let you go free for the last time, Cousin."

A couple of men came in with a granite statue he'd sent them to bring from the courtyard. He grabbed the end and motioned for them to back up and charge the door. They had to repeat the action a half dozen times before the frame gave. From the lack of threats while they were trying to break into the room, he already knew what he would find.

Nothing.

Cold panic spread in his stomach.

The room had no windows. Majid was paranoid that way. With reason. Anyone who ruled by fear was bound to make enemies.

Saeed unlocked the two other doors and found his own men facing him, weapons drawn. He stepped back into the room, banged on the walls, looking for a hidden exit. "There has to be a passageway."

His men rushed to the search, one of them yelling out his discovery a few minutes later.

No time to find the opening mechanism. Saeed kicked in the panel then ran forward. They had precious little time to waste. If they weren't late already. No, he could not think that. He could not accept even the possibility that his loved ones might be dead.

They reached the morgue, and he had his men check the vaults in the wall. He didn't breathe until they had gone through every last one.

His limbs felt numb, his chest as if a herd of camels trampled over it.

"Spread out." He rushed from the room, knowing too much time had passed. They were unlikely to find Majid here.

He ran through the basement and up the stairs, bumping into one of his men.

"They left through the ambulance bay."

He followed the man, scanned the dead left on the concrete floor, lying in their own blood, and was relieved that neither his son, nor his sisters, nor Dara were among them.

"Go, send our people out into the city. Pass the word. Every ambulance must be stopped," he said, then pulled out his cell phone to call Nasir.

"Majid has Salah and our sisters, Dara, too. He's on his way out of the city." He explained the details as he ran from the building.

Once on the street, he grabbed a car from one of his men and raced over the asphalt, watching for any sign of them from behind the madly working windshield wipers. The sun was coming up behind the clouds, the streets lighter now. Rain poured from the sky, the city smelling sweet and wet, filled with hope as he was filled with despair.

Where would Majid go? He would have to leave the city, too many of the opposition were there right now. He would go somewhere he would feel safe. His southern troops?

Saeed turned the car down the boulevard and pushed the gas pedal to the floor. He didn't slow when his cell phone rang, but kept the steering wheel steady with one hand while he answered it.

"Someone came across an abandoned ambulance in the East Souq. I'm on my way over," Nasir said.

"Me, too." He took a sharp turn toward the market, and beeped at a group of women to get out of the way.

He was four blocks away, made it there in under two minutes. Then it took a while to find the ambulance, wedged within the labyrinth of tables. At least the market was empty. Every able-bodied man was at the palace today.

He saw his men surround the vehicle with guns drawn, stopped the car and ran toward them, straight for the doors. Locked.

He called out his son's name.

No response.

"Dara? Fatima? Lamis?"

His heart hammered against his chest. He barely noticed the rain that ran down his face and soaked his clothes. One of his men ran to him with a crowbar. He grabbed it and wedged it between the doors.

They popped open, and air returned to his lungs once he saw Salah and his sisters on the floor, bound and gagged, but alive.

He pulled out his knife and freed them, hugging them, not ever wanting to let go.

"Are you all right? Did he hurt you?" he asked when they finally separated.

Fatima and Lamis shook their heads. Salah held on to Saeed's leg tight enough to cut off his circulation. They were safe. Relief washed through him in waves. But he had more work to do, a piece of his heart still missing.

"Where is Dara?"

Fatima filled him in, so scared and shaken she made little sense. It took a while to calm her and get all the details.

"What happened to Gedad?"

She shook her head. "We never made it that far."

"I'll take care of our family," Nasir said from behind Saeed. "Majid is gone, you are the king. You must return to the palace and restore order."

King, he thought surprised. Nasir was right.

Majid had fled the capital. His cousin's despotic reign was over.

"You need to show your strength, order the cabinet to meet at once," Nasir pressed.

"No." He looked his brother in the eye, wanting to make sure Nasir understood him. "Not while my queen is missing."

He squatted in front of Salah. "I'm proud of you for being so brave, son."

He gave the boy a long hug, thanking Allah for returning his only child to him. Then he ran to the car. Majid would go to the desert. He'd be recognized if he drove through the towns and villages. He wouldn't trust the people who were rising up against him.

Saeed hit the steering wheel with his open palm. He would not let Dara come to harm. He would protect her whatever the price. There were people she trusted, people who could help her.

He flipped his cell phone open, scanned the saved list of the last ten numbers dialed and found the one he was looking for—the call to the U.S. He dialed the numbers, keeping an eye on the road ahead of him.

"Hello," a man answered without identifying himself.

"This is Sheik Saeed ibn Ahmad. Dara Alexander was taken hostage by King Majid."

A brief silence followed his words.

"Any ideas on her location?"

"Somewhere in the desert not far from Tihrin. Most likely a single truck with a handful of guards, heading away from the city."

"Keep this line open," the man said and clicked off.

He drove on to the sound of rain drumming on the car roof, and prayed that she was still alive. She was strong, she would not back down from Majid. She would try to fight him, try to escape. Fear shrank his chest cavity, making it hard to breathe. Majid would not put up with resistance.

If he touched her, if he harmed her in any way… Saeed drove on, barely seeing the road in front of him.

He was on the outskirts of the city when the phone rang.

"I'm looking at the latest satellite pictures," the man said. "There's a truck heading toward an oasis about two hundred miles west from Tihrin. It's in a deep valley. There's a small armed force there. Are you authorizing U.S. assistance?"

"Yes," he said without hesitation. "Do whatever is necessary to save her."

"The nearest air force base is in somewhat of an upheaval, but I can get a chopper to her within the next hour or so."

Saeed closed the phone and stepped on the gas. He knew the oasis the man was talking about—a small well that was insufficient for watering entire herds, but frequented by gun and drug smugglers alike.

They liked its geography, the thousand-meter-high sand dunes that surrounded it, making it an easily defendable location in case of attack.

DARA SHOOK THE RAINWATER out of her hair as she walked back into the empty tent, eager to get away from the leering of the royal guard. They had allowed her out, but did not give her the privacy to go to the bathroom. She tried to pretend it didn't bother her.

Her boots were covered with wet sand. She pulled out her knife and slid it up her sleeve, taking advantage of being alone for the first time since they had arrived at camp.

She didn't have a good feeling about the place, nor the people—three dozen men, armed to the teeth, silent and menacing. They gave Majid shelter, but she got the impression they weren't crazy about it. They probably figured sooner or later someone would come after the king.

She looked up as Majid entered and sat on the carpet across from her, staring at her. She nearly smiled. A lucky break at last.

"I can see why my cousin found you refreshing." He rubbed his palms on his knees. "You must have given him a wild ride."

Rain drummed on the canvas above her head. She didn't respond. Her mind was on the handgun tucked into the man's belt.

"I myself am a connoisseur of Western women." He spread and stretched his legs. "When I'm done with him, Saeed will be nothing. I'll still be king."

He pulled out his gun with his right hand. With his left hand, he undid his belt and unzipped his pants.

"I thought the sanctity of women was one of the most important values of your people."

"The *sharaf,* yes. Sanctity of *our* women. You're not Saeed's wife. You're his foreign whore."

He motioned her closer with the gun, as one of his guards came through the flap. Majid said something, and the man backed out.

She stood slowly, pretending reluctance, then stopped.

His face contorted. "I'm still king. I will be obeyed."

She stepped toward him and placed herself between his legs. He grabbed her wrist with his left hand and yanked her to her knees. *Now.* She twisted her hand around, grabbed onto his wrists hard enough to make him drop the gun, while with her other hand she went for her knife and had it at his throat the next second.

"The single biggest mistake one can make in war," she said with a smile as she picked up his pistol, "is to underestimate the enemy."

Red fury spread from his neck up his face. "You will regret this," he hissed the words. "I will personally make sure you die in pain."

"I don't think that'll happen." She put the gun to his head and tucked her knife away, pulling him to his feet. "But you can fantasize about it while you're in jail." She yanked his zipper up with just a touch of unnecessary force, not wanting his pants to drop and slow him down.

When she led him out of the tent into the rain, it took a second before his guards comprehended what had happened. Another second and their guns were trained on Dara.

She shook her head. "Drop them."

Nobody moved.

The men in the camp watched the scene with curiosity, but stayed away.

Majid said something in Arabic.

"Say one more word I don't understand and it will be your last." She shoved him toward the nearest truck.

Very much aware of the eight guns pointed at her heart, she made her way to the front of the vehicle slowly, opening the door without taking her eyes off the soldiers. She had to take Majid with her. Without him, his guards would shoot her into a sieve.

She hoped the king knew the way to the city. Having spent the journey so far in the back of the truck, she had no idea which way they had come, only that they had followed the wadi here. She'd seen that every time one of the guards had opened the canvas flap to check if anyone was catching up with them.

With the gun at Majid's head, she shoved the man up behind the wheel, then over to the passenger side, making room for herself. She started the truck, turned it, never moving the pistol from his temple.

She kept an eye on his men who kept their rifles trained at her, stepped on the gas like she meant it, then drove out of the valley and took the truck down into the wadi. There was some muddy water on the bottom, not much, a couple of inches at most.

A car emerged from behind the tall sand dunes to follow her on the bank. She didn't like that, them having higher position. It gave them an advantage. She stepped on the gas, but the truck wasn't going nearly as fast as she would have liked, the wadi bottom getting slippery and sticky with mud. It seemed the guards on the bank were having the same problem. They had trouble closing the distance between them.

She hadn't gotten ten miles from camp when she realized she had to get out of the wadi as soon as she could. She turned the wheel then swore as the tires spun out when the truck tried to climb the incline. She needed both hands on the wheel, but couldn't afford to take the gun off Majid.

The truck slid back to the bottom. Fine. The water was still only about six inches deep, nothing the vehicle couldn't handle. She would drive on until she reached a spot where the bank wasn't as steep as here.

Helicopters flew overhead. Black Hawks, she recognized their distinctive sound. She stuck her head out the window but couldn't see the birds from the bottom of the wadi.

"We have to get out," Majid said, the anger in his voice tinged with fear.

"Not yet." She kept the gun on him.

She could see just the spot a few hundred feet ahead and pushed forward. She turned the wheel carefully when they got there, gave the motor more gas. They were making it.

But they didn't make it far before the tires spun out on the muddy incline and the truck began to slide back, pulled by its own weight.

"Damn." She tried again.

It didn't work.

And they couldn't get out of the vehicle. They weren't far enough from Majid's guards. She could not allow them to catch up. She had to get away from the men and their semiautomatics.

She backed down to the wadi bottom, thinking she would go forward some more, find a better spot to get out, but the water was up to the top of the tires now. God, it was rising fast. Once it reached the motor they'd be screwed. She drove forward a few hundred feet, tried again, but got stuck.

For good this time. The loose sand had mixed into mud on the side of the wadi and trapped the wheels.

"Stupid, stupid woman, you will kill us both." Majid swore and berated her some more.

"Shut up." She tried to switch from forward to reverse, rock the truck out of the bad spot. It dug in deeper.

The rain was getting louder. Not the rain. She looked up just as Majid said, "Allah be merciful."

A wall of water raced toward them, frothy with anger, carrying bushes and entire palm trees on its back.

Holy heavens. For a split second she considered whether it was safer to stay in the truck or try to swim for it. She decided on the latter, thinking the force of the water was going to roll the truck something fierce. She didn't want to get trapped inside.

"Out!" She shoved the gun she'd stolen from Majid into her waistband, and went for her door, made it no more than a couple of yards up the bank in the slippery mud before the water reached them.

She slipped, fell, then was carried away at a frightening speed. A palm tree rushed by her but she couldn't grab on. She saw Majid close to her right. He went under, came up again, latched on to a good chunk of driftwood.

It took all her strength to keep her head above water. She tried to angle herself toward the edge of the wadi that was now a three-hundred-foot-wide rolling river, but didn't make much progress.

She chucked the gun and her boots, not wanting anything to pull her down, but she still got tumbled under. An eternity passed before she could claw her way up to the rolling surface and cough the sandy water out of her lungs. If her situation wasn't so desperate, she would have laughed at how bizarre it all was.

She was drowning in the middle of the desert.

She saw a handful of the royal guards up on the bank as the water rushed her by them. When the water spun her around for a second, she could see them running along the edge of the wadi, yelling what was probably encouragement to their king.

Her muscles were growing weak from the desperate struggle. She fought against the current, getting a little closer to shore, although not on her own effort but by chance, pushed by the unpredictable waters.

Except that now there was an obstacle in her way. A giant boulder loomed a couple of hundred feet ahead, directly in her path. She put all her strength into trying to swim, trying to give her movements some direction. If she smashed against it, she was done.

The water rushed her forward with amazing speed. She put everything she had into reaching shore, but everything she had was not enough. At the last second she pulled her legs up in front of her, and bent her knees. Then she hit.

The position absorbed most of the shock. She latched on to the boulder, refused to go under.

She wasn't going to drown, damn it.

She tried to drag herself up but the pull of the water was too strong. She struggled to find a foothold. After an eternity, she finally did. Her thigh muscles trembled as she pushed up, found an outcropping to grab onto, then lifted her upper body out of the water.

Rain pounded her face but she ignored it as she ignored the cold that wanted to suck away what little remaining strength she had in her body.

Her fingertips were bleeding by the time she made it to the top of the boulder, roughly three feet above water level, a safe spot for now. Until the river rose higher.

She saw the royal guard running down the bank. Then she spotted Majid's dark head in the water. The current seemed to push him toward his men, and they held their rifles out for him.

She watched him struggle before he caught one, only to have it slip out of his fingers. But he was lucky; a second later he grabbed on to another and this time he was able to hang on.

As much as she disliked the man, she did not wish for him to drown. Having gotten so close to a watery death herself—and still not completely clear of it— she couldn't wish that on anyone. But it burned her that he would be getting away, after what he had done to Saeed and his own people.

When his men finally pulled Majid out, he

sprawled on his back in the mud, gasping for air. She knew how he felt.

Then one of the guards spotted her and yelled something. Even over the rain and the noise of the churning water she could hear the triumph in the man's voice as he raised his rifle.

Chapter Eleven

Dara threw herself on her stomach. This was the end. She could not go back into the water, and up here she had nowhere to hide. Still, at least it would be death by a bullet and not by drowning. All in all she preferred it this way. But it galled her to go out like this, defenseless. She would have given anything for a gun, to be able to take at least some of those bastards with her.

She flinched as the first shots rang out and bounced off the rock a few inches from her. As a soldier, she was used to being under fire, but this was different. This was target practice. Being the target wasn't a comfortable feeling. Screw them. She raised her middle finger and waved it in the air.

They responded with more bullets. *How predictable.*

She thought of Saeed, his smile, his mesmerizing blue eyes, the time they had spent in the cave, riding

Hawk in the desert in the moonlight. Whatever little time she had left, she wanted to spend with him, even if only in her imagination. She hoped he had found his sisters and Salah by now and they were all safe.

She loved him.

The admission scared her as much as the bullets that buzzed like angry bees around her, maybe more. But staring death in the face brought her feelings into sharp focus, and there was little point in denying them. She had fallen in love with the future king of Beharrain.

Love wasn't something she'd ever seen in her parents' marriage, and she had been convinced it would be impossible to find in her line of work, anyway. But here she was, in love. In a way, she was glad to have gotten this unexpected gift, to know what love was before she died.

Another spray of bullets hit close to her face and she pulled her head down to protect herself from the flying shards of stone.

And then she heard more shots, but coming from a distance. Then more and more and more.

She lifted her head and blinked at the sight of dozens of vehicles flying through the rain over the muddy sand. Camels? She blinked her eyes. Yes, Bedu warriors on camels behind cars. The scene was bizarre, an updated version of *Lawrence of Arabia*.

They reached Majid and his guards fast and surrounded them. Her heart stopped for a moment when she recognized the man who stepped out of the car in the lead.

Saeed.

She stood on the rock, yelled, waved, but it wasn't necessary. He had seen her already.

He had come to save her.

Relief coursed through her body. She was breathless, her mind reeling at having gone from sure death to seeing Saeed again. He had found her somehow.

He ran toward her, leaving Majid to his men. He found a palm trunk that had been wedged between the stones on the bank and freed it, holding on to one end while he floated the other out into the current. She could only stare at the superhuman feat. The tree trunk was a good twenty feet long, but he held its weight against the rushing water.

A dozen of Saeed's men were right behind him, helping now. She prayed as the water pushed the trunk toward the boulder. It was long enough, the end of it catching on the rocks. It held. Her muscles went weak with relief. But she couldn't relax yet. She scooted over and lowered her feet into the river.

"Stay where you are," Saeed shouted and jumped in, disappeared under the frothy water.

She didn't breathe until his head broke the surface again.

She watched him struggle with the current, hanging on to the palm trunk that was anchored by her boulder on one end and by his people on the other. He should have tied a rope around his waist. Of course, he probably didn't have a rope. Or he didn't want to waste time, fearing the water would rise and sweep her away. It reached almost to the top of the boulder now.

Then a terrible possibility occurred to her—if the water washed over the rock, it would lift the end of the log and take it. The current was strong enough to rip the other end from the men's hands. And then both Saeed and she would be lost.

She kept her eyes on him as she slipped into the river and moved forward with renewed desperation, gripping the log, frustrated at how little progress she was making. The water battled against them, but they held on, never taking their gazes off each other. When they finally met in the middle, he held a hand out, and she slipped into his embrace, feeling his strong arm slide around her and hold her to him.

And for a moment they clung together, her head buried in the nook of his shoulder, relief shaking her body.

"Are you okay?"

She looked up into clear blue eyes that seemed to see to her soul and nodded. "Let's get out of here."

They made their way back in the lashing rain,

hanging on to each other and to the palm trunk. When one slipped for a moment, the other pulled harder.

They were within three feet of shore when the palm trunk shook and swung around. The men held fast, yelling at them in panic. Saeed grabbed her tight, then let go of the log and heaved his body toward the bank, pulling her with him through the rolling current.

Water rushed into her lungs. She coughed, clawed forward, reaching nothing solid she could grab onto. She swam for all she was worth, refusing to give up. They were not going to die. Not today, damn it.

Then they were pulled up by a dozen seeking hands. She lay on the shore and gasped for air, still dizzy from the effort when Saeed lifted her into his arms and walked away from the river's edge with her.

The movement triggered something in her body and she heaved water out of her lungs. "Sorry," she managed to say, embarrassed.

He held her tighter and pressed his lips to the top of her head.

SHE WAS SAFE. Saeed took the first full, relaxed breath since the double golden doors had closed behind Dara. She was safe. His heart had nearly burst with fear when he had driven over the dunes and saw her on that boulder with bullets flying around her.

If he had lost her… He couldn't even think about that. She was his heart.

He carried her toward the car, pausing when they passed by Majid and the man spoke to him.

"Cousin, I was coming back to ask for your understanding and forgiveness."

"You must ask our people," Saeed responded. "You can ask them when you stand trial."

"You cannot put me on trial. I'm of royal blood," he said, looking shocked. "I'm of *your* blood." The last words came out laced with anger.

"You committed many crimes against the people. You must answer to them."

"I will go into exile."

"If the people so decide." Saeed inclined his head. "But I don't think they will."

He watched his cousin's face turn redder by the moment, saw his snap of control, remained motionless when Majid lurched against the men who held him fast.

"I should have taken care of you when I took care of your father." Majid spat the venomous words.

Saeed let Dara slip to the ground, his peripheral vision narrowed, his entire being focused now on the man in front of him.

"You were responsible for my father's death?" He barely recognized his own voice, so cold it could have turned the rain to hail.

Majid just grinned at him, the pleasure of causing pain obvious on his face. Then Saeed stepped closer and the look on his cousin's face turned more serious.

He could murder him. He wanted to—here and now.

He felt Dara's touch on his arm, a tenuous link to reason.

He glanced around at his men and saw his anger and outrage mirrored in their eyes. They would not have disapproved if he ripped Majid's throat out with his bare hands. He was the victim's son, the blood revenge his right according to the Bedu code that was hundreds of years older than any written law of the land.

Dara's hand tightened on him. He took a deep breath. By tomorrow this time he would be king, sworn to uphold the laws of the country. But today, right now, the urge to harm the man in front of him was overwhelming.

"Saeed." Dara's voice reached him through the fog of anger.

He turned to look at her, and her troubled gaze was like a slap on the skin.

He stepped away from Majid. If he were to be king, he would be a just king or not take the throne at all.

"Take him to the palace prison," he said to his men as he strode away in the rain.

Dara was by his side. "What was that about?"

The words hurt on their way out. "He killed my father."

She glanced back at Majid then at Saeed, anger and sympathy mixing in her eyes. "Nasir was right. I'm sorry."

He nodded and squeezed her hand. He loved having her beside him.

"Did you find Salah and your sisters?" she asked in a transparent attempt to distract him.

"They are with Nasir." She was right. That's what he needed to focus on. His family was safe, Dara was safe. "Thank you for what you did for them."

"You're welcome." She glanced at Majid as he was being led away. "It is over, the throne is yours."

And it hit him that it *was* over. He was safe from Majid. Her mission in Beharrain was done.

But there was no way he could let her go.

The sound of helicopters filled the air. The U.S. rescue, he thought. They must have figured out when they got to the oasis that Dara had already escaped.

And through the rain, he saw trucks heading toward him, a half dozen or so. They were fleeing from the Americans.

When they got closer, the trucks stopped and the men got out. They were Beharrainians, he could tell at a glimpse from the distinctive curve of their daggers.

"We come in peace, brother," their leader said. "We ask for your protection from the foreign dogs."

Saeed watched two helicopters land behind the men who were moving toward him. The well-armed group wanted to melt into the sea of two thousand warriors who stood behind Saeed, thanks to Nasir who had alerted the tribes in the area to join him.

"Allah be praised, we found you," the leader said not more than ten meters away now.

Saeed watched the men, the military trucks behind them that did not belong to the country's army. He knew who they were—terrorists, lawless, honorless men whom his cousin had tolerated in the country to do his dirty work for him.

Smug relief spread across the leader's face. He knew the two dozen U.S. soldiers behind them could not stand up to Saeed's force.

Saeed watched as the men came closer still. They were Beharrainian; he owed them his protection from the foreigners. They were his blood.

No, he thought then. They had betrayed that blood. He had nothing in common with them. They were cowards and murderers. They were probably the very people who had attacked the U.S. Air Force base in Saudi.

He signaled to his men and the next second their weapons were raised. The terrorists froze, confusion and anger on their faces. They swore and threatened, but did not open fire—they knew when they were faced with an overwhelming force.

"Come." Saeed turned to Dara. "Let's go talk to your people and see what we can do to make sure justice prevails."

"You called in the U.S.?" Her ebony eyes were round with surprise.

"When I thought I might lose you—" A cold fist squeezed his chest when he thought of it even now. He cleared his throat. "I realized how insane it was to argue over who is doing what when we have the same purpose. If you were hurt because of my pride, I would have never forgiven myself."

"I'm tougher than I look," she said with a smile that lit up her beautiful face.

"I know," he said. "But maybe I'm not. Not when it comes to you."

DARA SOAKED in the luxurious pool in the guest room of Saeed's house in Tihrin, enjoying the hot water that was beginning finally to take the chill out of her.

She closed her eyes and tried to relax. She had done it. She had given her resignation to the Colonel over the phone. Sometime soon she would have to go back for a debriefing and to sign the paperwork, but otherwise she was free. The Colonel hadn't been overexcited, but wished her the best, and consoled himself with having some crucial new information on the gun trade, and a number of wanted terrorists in custody.

She was officially out of the military.

Strangely, the thought did not fill her with panic. For the first time in her life, the abundance of possibilities filled her with excitement instead of fear. She knew who she was. She would not lose her way like her mother had.

For the foreseeable future, she would stay in Beharrain, help organize foreign aid, spend some time with the Bedu perhaps. Saeed had mentioned bringing his ancestors' treasure to Tihrin and opening a museum. The thought appealed to her. She could help with that.

There were a hundred ways she could be useful and stay near him. And she wanted that above all, in any capacity he was willing to accept. God, she was pitiful. No, she corrected, she was a woman in love wanting to stay with the man she loved.

Eventually, she would deal with the fact that she could never have him fully. She was strong.

Salah's words floated back to her from when they had first met. *Father will marry for alliance between the tribes. He can't marry a foreigner. It wouldn't be any use at all.*

She imagined it was even truer now. Kings did not marry for love, probably not even in this day and age.

She looked up at the sound of the door opening and smiled at the sight of Saeed, more bedraggled than she'd ever seen him, and still heartachingly handsome. Even when wet.

"Still raining?"

He nodded, his pleasure with the weather written all over his face. "With a good rain like this, the Bedu herds will have enough grazing for the next two or three years."

He shed his clothes as he came over, making her pulse speed, making her laugh with joy when he slipped into the water next to her.

He took her hands, kissed her bruised fingertips. "Are you okay?"

She soaked up his undivided attention. "All in a day's work." She smiled when he frowned, liking that he felt protective about her. "Unfortunately, as of a couple of hours ago, I'm unemployed."

He went still, his gaze searched his face. "Are you sure this is what you want to do? I hate seeing you in any kind of danger, but if that's what makes you happy, I would not ever ask you to give it up."

You make me happy.

"I'm sure. I think I might stay here for a while." The country and its people had captured her heart, which ached for the Bedu and their slowly disappearing ways. She felt a kinship toward Saeed's people that she couldn't explain. "There's a lot to do. Maybe I can help."

The dazzling smile that split his face chased all her

insecurities away. He leaned forward and brushed his lips against hers gently. She moved into the circle of his arms and it felt good and right, pleasure filling her when he deepened the kiss.

She let herself be swept away by the sensation. He was here, with her. That it was temporary didn't matter, because for this brief moment in time she felt complete, perfectly happy.

He pulled away, looked her in the eye.

"I love you," he said.

And she could only blink as the question she had carried around for most of her life was finally answered. With sudden clarity, she finally knew where she belonged. She belonged with Saeed, whether they were in the middle of the desert in a rainstorm or in Tihrin or Baltimore. They belonged together.

That's what she wanted more than anything else in the world and, damn it, she couldn't have it. Tomorrow he would be king.

She could be his mistress, forever if they both wanted it, a small voice said in her mind. But then something, perhaps the pride of the Lenape rose inside her, and she knew she would not settle. Nor would she give up.

She was no longer a soldier, but she still knew how to fight. And what they could have was worth fighting for. It was worth everything.

"I love you, too." She dipped her lips back to his and they drank love until they were both drunk with it.

When they finally came up for air again, he lifted her legs to wrap around his waist. And all of a sudden she found it difficult to focus on making her case.

"I have to get back to the palace soon," he said. "I have to make sure the army is under control and will accept my command." He nibbled the sensitive skin on her neck. "There will be a ceremony to make everything official. Probably first thing tomorrow. I want to push things along so the country can return to normal as soon as possible."

She nodded and wondered if her own life would ever return to normal again.

He stopped the wicked things he was doing to her body and looked her straight in the eye. "I have no right to ask this…"

He was going to ask her to be his permanent bodyguard. "Yes," she said without thinking. It would keep them close and give her a chance to convince him they had something together.

A slow smile spread on his face. His shoulders relaxed. "You'll be my queen?"

She stared at him, stunned, the air stolen from her lungs. "Queen?" she squeaked.

He narrowed his eyes. "What did you think I was offering?"

"A job?"

"Well, someone told me not so long ago that I was a piece of work." He smiled again with mischief in his eyes.

"Whoever she was, she must have had amazing insight." She returned the smile, feeling like she was floating on top of pink clouds.

"Will you marry me?" Banked fire burned in his gaze.

She forgot to breathe.

"I'm hopelessly in love with you," he said with wonder in his voice. "It might sound strange, but sometimes I look at you and it's as if I've known you for years."

"Forever," she said, and he nodded. She knew the feeling well. "I love you, too. And I will marry you."

He smiled at her, his brilliant blue eyes sparkling with love. He kissed her again, and she let herself get lost in the pleasure of him.

"I worried all afternoon that you would say no," he said when they pulled apart. "I wasn't sure I could let you go. It would have looked bad if the first thing I did as king was kidnap a foreign national."

She laughed, loving the playful tone of his voice, that the dark shadow of stress had finally lifted.

"I thought for sure you would marry for alliance," she admitted, giddy with relief now that that was cleared up. She kissed the corner of his mouth.

"Maybe the second or third wives. The Koran allows four so I have three more chances to make alliances. Ouch," he said when she bit his lip.

He pulled back to look her in the eye. "My heart belongs to you, Dara," he said with all seriousness. "I will never love another."

She ran her fingers up his chest and couldn't help flashing him a wicked grin. "Just to be on the safe side, I'm going to make sure you won't have enough energy for one." She thoroughly enjoyed watching his eyes darken with passion.

"You will be the one and only for me, forever. I will put it in a marriage contract if you want and seal it with the grand seal of the king. You are my heart, you complete my life. We were meant for each other from the beginning of time."

His words sneaked around her heart and sent her spirit soaring. She was home, she thought for the first time in her life. This is where she had been heading all along. Home was where you were happy. She was happy here with him.

Epilogue

"I didn't realize a museum opening could be so exhausting." Dara closed her eyes for a moment and let Saeed peel off the layers of silk and muslin from her body. She enjoyed her involvement in saving a large part of Bedu history. She enjoyed pretty much everything about her new position, the opportunities it provided her to do good and make a difference.

Her work was not as public as some first ladies' of the West, but the country was accepting her for who she was. Besides the museum that was a project close to her heart, she had many others, aimed at women and children. Even the religious fanatics tended to overlook that as long as she didn't involve herself in things they considered strictly men's territory.

She didn't mind. There were plenty of Beharrainian children and women who needed her help. Thank God, she wasn't alone. She'd been pleasantly surprised at how many people had sought her out over the last few months, offering either financial support for her initiatives or volunteering for one of her projects. None with a more impressive track record than Dr. Abigail DiMatteo-Logan, the tireless mother of the most gorgeous six-month-old Dara had seen. Abigail had started a novel program for war orphans that was beginning to be copied throughout the country.

With time, things would change. Beharrain had a very open-minded ruler. Dara liked that about him.

He caressed her breasts with the hands of an angel as they lay on the bed. She liked that about him, too.

"You're tired. Why don't you rest for a while?" He moved away and started to work on his own clothing.

She turned to her side, watching him discard his underwear. Her pulse quickened. "Sleep sounds good," she said. "In a while."

He looked into her eyes, his lips curving into a slow smile when he read her desire. "I hoped you would say that."

He sat next to her on the bed and pulled her onto his lap, gazing into her eyes with a sudden gravity. "Are you sure it doesn't bother you that after me, Salah will be king, not your sons?"

"Sons? What if we have daughters? The ultrasound showed only the two heartbeats. It's too early to tell the sex."

"You know what I mean," he said, searching her face.

She hadn't realized he had been concerned about this. "If we have any boys they'll be princes. I think I can live with that."

"But Salah will be crown prince."

"He is my son, too, you know."

"Ya noori," he said. You are my light.

"And you, mine."

He kissed her then, long and slow, laid her on her back. A lump of something hard pressed against her skull.

"What's that?" She patted her pillow.

He reached under it, pulled out a small leather sack with a black silk cord, the leather decorated with turquoise beads in a breathtaking floral pattern. It looked familiar.

He dropped it into her hand. "A small gift."

"Another one?" She peeked inside the bag and caught a glimpse of gold. In a way that was most undignified for a queen, she squealed in delight. "I wondered where that went. When I did the inventory for the museum it was conspicuously missing."

"So you've been looking for it?" His sexy lips stretched into a wide grin. "I'm glad you like it. But to be fair, in the interest of cultural exchange, at one point I think you should show me some Lenape tricks."

And when he looked at her like that, she didn't have the heart to tell him that her knowledge of Lenape tricks consisted of running the blackjack table and operating the cash register at the tax-free ciga-rette shop. She had a strong suspicion that wasn't what he had in mind.

"For the sake of cultural exchange," she said and lifted her lips to his.

She had a good idea what kind of tricks he was looking for. And never one to disappoint, she was willing to make up some.

* * * * *

Don't miss Dana Marton's next
gripping tale featuring members of the
SDDU when CAMOUFLAGE HEART
hits shelves in October 2005!

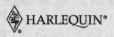
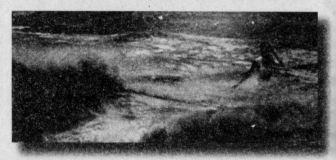

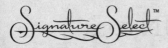

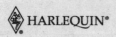
HARLEQUIN®

INTRIGUE®

As the summer comes to a close, things really begin to heat up as Harlequin Intrigue presents…

Big Sky Bounty Hunters: No man's a match for these Montana tough guys…but a woman's another story.

Don't miss this brand-new series from some of your favorite authors!

GOING TO EXTREMES
BY AMANDA STEVENS
August 2005

BULLSEYE
BY JESSICA ANDERSEN
September 2005

WARRIOR SPIRIT
BY CASSIE MILES
October 2005

FORBIDDEN CAPTOR
BY JULIE MILLER
November 2005

RILEY'S RETRIBUTION
BY RUTH GLICK,
writing as Rebecca York
December 2005

Available at your favorite retail outlet.